The Chocolate Bunny Murders

An Easter Cozy Mystery

When a chocolatier is found dead, it's up to a local detective to crack the case

Holly Winters

Copyright © 2025 Holly Winters
All rights reserved

No part of this book may be reproduced, stored in a retrieval system, or transmitted in any form or by any means, electronic, mechanical, photocopying, recording, or otherwise, without the prior written permission of the publisher, except in the case of brief quotations embodied in critical articles and reviews.

This is a work of fiction. Names, characters, places, and incidents either are the product of the author's imagination or are used fictitiously. Any resemblance to actual persons, living or dead, businesses, companies, events, or locales is entirely coincidental.

Contents

chapter 1: Sweet Beginnings, Bitter Endings 7

Chapter 2: Melting Alibis 21

Chapter 3: Bitter Truths 40

Chapter 4: Cracked Shells 58

Chapter 5: Dark Chocolate Secrets 78

Chapter 6: The Final Bite 94

Chapter 7: Sweet Justice 113

Thank You To Readers 137

Chapter 1: Sweet Beginnings, Bitter Endings

The scent of chocolate hung thick in the air as I piped a delicate pattern along the ears of what had to be my hundredth chocolate bunny of the day. My fingers ached from the repetitive motion, but there was no time to rest. Easter was less than two weeks away, and Heavenly Confections—the chocolate shop I ran with my aunt Nettie—was drowning in orders.

"Lee, what do you think? Too much sparkle?"

I looked up to see my aunt holding a tray of completed bunnies, each dusted with edible gold shimmer that caught the light streaming through our shop windows. At sixty-two, Aunt Nettie still had the enthusiasm of someone half her age, especially when it came to holiday-themed confections.

"Not possible," I said, setting down my piping bag. "Easter is all about rebirth and celebration. Sparkle away."

She beamed at me, the fine lines around her eyes crinkling with pleasure. "That's what I told Mrs. Henderson when she called this morning asking if we could make her order 'more sophisticated.' Since when are chocolate bunnies supposed to be sophisticated?"

"Since Abigail Thornton decided our Easter festival needed to appeal to the weekend tourists from the city," I replied, rolling my shoulders to release the tension. "Speaking of which, did you finish the special order for the committee meeting tonight?"

Aunt Nettie nodded toward the refrigerated display case. "Front and center. Twelve specialty bunnies with the festival logo emblazoned on their tummies. Though I still think it's ridiculous that Abigail insisted they be done two weeks early just for a planning meeting."

"That's Abigail for you—"

A tremendous crash from the kitchen interrupted my thought, followed by a string of colorful apologies that would have made the Easter Bunny's ears curl. Aunt Nettie and I exchanged a knowing look.

"I'll go," I sighed, already untying my chocolate-smudged apron.

In the kitchen, surrounded by a sea of scattered cocoa powder and what appeared to be the remains of our delivery of chocolate molds, stood Bunny Birdsong—our newest employee and possibly the clumsiest human being I had ever encountered.

"Oh, Lee, I'm so sorry!" Bunny's round face crumpled as she clutched a now-empty cardboard box to her chest. Her floral scarf—which she wore regardless of the weather or practicality—was dusted with cocoa, making her look like she'd been caught in some bizarre chocolate sandstorm. "I was trying to reach the new Easter egg molds, but the bunny box was on top, and then everything just . . . just. . ."

"Decided to jump off the shelf and commit suicide?" I suggested with a wry smile.

Bunny's shoulders slumped further, if that was possible. "I'll clean it up right away. And I'll stay late to make up for the lost molds. And I'll pay for them out of my check. And I'll—"

I held up a hand to stem the tide of promises. "Take a breath, Bunny. It's just chocolate. No one died."

Her already wide eyes somehow managed to widen further as she nodded vigorously, sending a small cloud of cocoa powder into the air from her platinum blonde bob.

Bunny Birdsong had only been working at Heavenly Confections for three weeks. Despite her unfortunate propensity for disaster, there was something endearing about her eagerness to please. Plus, she had an almost supernatural ability to calm irate customers with her sweet, slightly scattered demeanor. I couldn't count the number of times a harried mother or irritated businessman had walked in ready to complain about a late order, only to leave ten minutes later smiling, with Bunny's enthusiastic assurances that their chocolate would be "absolutely perfect, just you wait and see!"

"Why don't you go help Aunt Nettie with the counter?" I suggested gently. "I think Mrs. Peabody is coming in to pick up her order for the church luncheon."

Relief flooded Bunny's face. "I can do that. Mrs. Peabody loves me. She says I remind her of her granddaughter." She paused, brow furrowing slightly. "Though I'm not sure if that's a compliment, since she also mentioned her granddaughter just got kicked out of her third college..."

"I'm sure she meant it in the best possible way," I assured her, already reaching for the broom. "Just . . . try not to knock over the display case."

"I would never!" Bunny gasped, then promptly backed into a rack of cooling trays, which wobbled ominously before settling. She shot me an apologetic grimace and scurried out to the front of the shop.

I shook my head, unable to suppress a smile as I swept up the mess. In the three years since I'd returned to Sweetwater Springs to help Aunt Nettie run the family business, I'd grown accustomed to the rhythm of small-town life. The predictable flow of regular customers, the seasonal rushes, the gossip that spread faster than melted chocolate on a hot day. After my divorce from Richard—the corporate lawyer who'd decided our marriage was less important than making partner—the consistency had been healing.

Even Bunny, with her chaos-inducing presence, had quickly become part of that comforting pattern. Her hiring had raised a few eyebrows in town, particularly because of her ongoing divorce from Beau Birdsong, whose family owned half the real estate in the county. But Aunt Nettie had been adamant. "That girl needs a fresh start," she'd insisted after Bunny's interview. "And we need extra hands for Easter."

As I dumped the chocolate-covered debris into the trash, the bell above the shop door jingled. Through the kitchen's swinging door, I could hear Bunny's cheerful greeting transform into something more hesitant.

"Oh! Ms. Thornton . . . what a surprise."

My stomach clenched. Abigail Thornton was not one of our regular drop-in customers. As the wealthiest resident of Sweetwater Springs and the head of practically every committee in town, Abigail preferred to send her assistant to pick up orders.

"Ms. Birdsong." Abigail's crisp voice carried clearly into the kitchen. "I see you've found employment befitting your . . . skill set."

I winced at the thinly veiled insult and hurried to finish cleaning up. Bunny might be a disaster in the kitchen, but she didn't deserve Abigail's particular brand of condescension.

"Is Lee available?" Abigail continued. "I need to discuss the chocolate fountain for the Easter festival. The committee has concerns about its . . . appropriateness."

"I'll get her right away!" Bunny's voice was unnaturally high. "Lee is just busy being amazing in the kitchen. Creating chocolate masterpieces. She's so talented, don't you think? Not like me. I'm still learning. But Lee is just—"

"A simple 'one moment' would suffice, Ms. Birdsong."

I pushed through the swinging door, wiping my hands on a towel. "Abigail, what a surprise," I echoed Bunny's greeting, but with considerably less warmth. "What's this about the chocolate fountain?"

Abigail Thornton stood ramrod straight in her impeccable pastel suit, her silver-streaked hair pulled back in a severe bun. At sixty-five, she had the posture of a ballet dancer and the smile of someone who'd just tasted something slightly rancid.

"Lee," she nodded curtly. "The committee feels that a chocolate fountain might be too . . . messy for our upscale Easter festival this year. We're trying to attract a better class of visitors from the city."

I felt my jaw tighten. The chocolate fountain had been the highlight of the festival for the past five years. Children and adults alike looked forward to it, and it had always been Heavenly Confections' contribution to the event.

"The fountain is a tradition, Abigail. People love it."

"Some people," she corrected with a thin smile. "The sort who don't mind their children running around with chocolate-smeared faces. But we're elevating the festival this year. Think artisanal. Sophisticated. Clean." She glanced meaningfully at Bunny, who was nervously adjusting her cocoa-dusted scarf.

Before I could respond, Aunt Nettie emerged from the back storage room with a beautifully packaged box. "Abigail! Perfect timing. Your special order for tonight's meeting is ready."

Abigail's attention shifted, her eyes lighting up with something close to warmth as she accepted the box. "Nettie, always reliable.

Unlike some people." Another pointed look at Bunny, who suddenly became very interested in straightening already-neat stacks of chocolate boxes.

"Will there be anything else?" I asked, struggling to keep my tone professional.

"Yes, actually," Abigail set the box on the counter and extracted a folder from her designer handbag. "I wanted to give you this personally."

I took the folder, flipping it open to reveal architectural renderings of what appeared to be a significant renovation of the town square—including the block where Heavenly Confections was located.

"What is this?"

"The future," Abigail announced with unmistakable satisfaction. "The town council will be voting next week on my proposal for the Sweetwater Springs Restoration Project. We'll be revitalizing the entire downtown area to attract more upscale businesses and tourists."

My eyes narrowed as I scanned the plans. "This shows our building completely remodeled. We rent this space, Abigail. We can't make these kinds of structural changes."

"Oh, you won't have to worry about that," she waved a dismissive hand. "My development company will be purchasing the building from old Mr. Jenkins. As your new landlord, we'll handle all the renovations. Of course, your rent will need to reflect the improvements."

I felt the blood drain from my face. "By 'reflect,' you mean increase. Substantially."

Abigail's smile didn't reach her eyes. "It's simply the cost of progress, dear. Sweetwater Springs can't stay frozen in time forever."

Bunny made a small, distressed sound, and I shot her a warning glance. The last thing we needed was for her to get involved in this conversation.

"This is the first I'm hearing about any of this," I said carefully, closing the folder. "Does Mr. Jenkins know you're planning to buy his building?"

"We're in the final stages of negotiation," Abigail replied smoothly. "I'm simply giving you a courtesy heads-up. As a prominent business in town, I thought you'd appreciate being informed before the public announcement."

"How thoughtful," I muttered.

Aunt Nettie stepped forward, her usually cheerful face now serious. "Abigail, we've been in this location for over forty years. My mother started this shop here. Lee grew up helping behind that very counter. Surely you understand what this place means to us and to the town."

For a moment, something like genuine regret flickered across Abigail's face. "Nettie, you know I respect tradition. But times change. If Heavenly Confections wants to survive, it needs to evolve too."

"Into what?" I demanded. "Some sterile, 'artisanal' boutique selling overpriced truffles to weekend tourists?"

Abigail's expression hardened. "Better that than becoming obsolete. Think about it, Lee. Change is coming whether you embrace it or not." She picked up her box of chocolates with a finality that signaled the end of the conversation. "I'll see you both at the committee meeting tonight. Seven o'clock sharp at the community center."

As the bell jingled to announce her departure, a heavy silence fell over the shop. I looked at Aunt Nettie, whose normally rosy complexion had paled considerably.

"Can she really do this?" I asked quietly.

Aunt Nettie sighed, suddenly looking every one of her sixty-two years. "If she buys the building, she can charge whatever rent she wants. And if we can't pay. . ." She let the sentence trail off, the implication hanging in the air between us.

"This is all my fault," Bunny blurted, startling us both. "She hates me, and now she's taking it out on you. I should quit. Then maybe she'll leave Heavenly Confections alone."

I frowned. "What are you talking about? Why would Abigail hate you?"

Bunny twisted her cocoa-dusted scarf nervously. "It's . . . complicated. Beau—my almost-ex-husband—he and Abigail have some kind of business arrangement. When I left him, she was furious. Said I was jeopardizing an important investment." Tears welled in her wide eyes. "I didn't understand what she meant then, but now. . ."

"Now you think she's targeting the shop because we hired you?" I finished incredulously.

Bunny nodded miserably. "She confronted me last week outside the grocery store. Said I'd regret crossing her and Beau."

Aunt Nettie and I exchanged concerned glances. "Why didn't you tell us this before?" I asked.

"I didn't want to cause more problems," Bunny whispered. "You've both been so kind to me. Giving me a job when no one else would. I thought if I just kept my head down, she'd forget about me eventually."

I felt a surge of protective anger. Whatever was happening between Bunny, her ex, and Abigail, it wasn't right for our business to be caught in the crossfire.

"Well, she's not getting away with this," I declared, slapping the folder down on the counter. "If Abigail thinks she can bully us out of business, she's got another thing coming."

"Lee," Aunt Nettie cautioned, "be careful. Abigail Thornton has a lot of influence in this town."

"So do we," I countered. "People love Heavenly Confections. They won't stand for her turning it into some pretentious chocolate boutique."

Bunny wiped her eyes, leaving smudges of cocoa on her cheeks. "What are you going to do?"

I grabbed my purse from under the counter, suddenly energized. "First, I'm going to talk to Mr. Jenkins. Then I'm going to make some calls. And tonight, I'll confront Abigail at the committee meeting."

"I'll come with you," Aunt Nettie declared. "Two Woodyards are better than one."

I nodded gratefully, then turned to Bunny. "Can you handle the shop for a couple of hours?"

Her eyes widened in panic. "Me? Alone? But what if I—"

"You'll be fine," I assured her, more confidently than I felt. "Just don't try to make anything. Sell what's in the cases, take orders, and call my cell if there's an emergency."

Bunny straightened her shoulders with determination. "I won't let you down, Lee. I promise."

"I know you won't," I said, giving her hand a quick squeeze. "And don't worry about Abigail. Whatever game she's playing, we'll figure it out."

As Aunt Nettie and I headed for the door, the bell jangled again, admitting Mrs. Peabody with her church group order list. Bunny immediately switched on her customer service charm, her earlier distress masked by a bright smile.

"Perfect timing, Mrs. Peabody! I have your order all ready to go..."

Outside on the sidewalk, I took a deep breath of the crisp spring air, trying to clear my head. The town square looked postcard-perfect, with pastel Easter decorations adorning every lamppost and storefront. Sweetwater Springs had been my home for most of my life, except for the ten years I'd spent trying to build a life with Richard in the city. I'd returned after our divorce, wounded but wiser, finding healing in the familiar rhythms of small-town life and the family business.

"She won't win this one," Aunt Nettie said firmly, as if reading my thoughts. "Heavenly Confections is more than just a chocolate shop. It's part of this town's heart."

I nodded, squaring my shoulders. "Let's go talk to Mr. Jenkins."

***

The rest of the afternoon passed in a blur of frustration. Mr. Jenkins wasn't home, his neighbor informing us he'd gone fishing for the day. Several calls to other business owners revealed that Abigail had approached many of them with similar "opportunities" to be part of her restoration project—although no one seemed entirely clear on what the project actually entailed beyond higher rents and fancy facades.

By the time we returned to the shop at closing time, my initial fire had dampened into smoldering concern. Abigail clearly had her tentacles deep into the town's business community. Fighting her wouldn't be easy.

To my relief, Heavenly Confections was still standing, with no obvious disasters having occurred in our absence. Bunny was helping the last customer, her animated descriptions of our chocolate-making process drawing delighted laughter from the young family.

After they left, she turned to us with a triumphant grin. "No catastrophes! Well, I did knock over the napkin display, but I put it back exactly as it was. Oh, and the phone rang seventeen times—I counted—but I wrote down all the messages." She thrust a notepad at me proudly.

"Seventeen calls in two hours?" I skimmed the notepad, noting that most were from regular customers concerned about rumors they'd heard regarding Heavenly Confections' future.

"Word travels fast," Aunt Nettie observed grimly.

"Like chocolate in a double boiler," I agreed. "Bunny, did anything else happen while we were gone?"

She bit her lip. "Well... Beau came by."

My head snapped up. "Your ex? What did he want?"

"To talk about Abigail, actually. He seemed really nervous." Bunny twisted her scarf—a nervous habit I was beginning to recognize. "He said he needed to warn me about something, but then two customers came in, and he left. Said he'd find me later."

That was interesting—and concerning. "Did he say what he wanted to warn you about?"

Bunny shook her head. "Just that Abigail was on the warpath and I should be careful. Which, honestly, isn't exactly breaking news." She hesitated. "There's something else... The vacant store next door? I saw someone go in there about an hour ago."

"Probably just the realtor," I said, distracted by the growing list of people I needed to talk to before the committee meeting.

"I don't think so," Bunny replied. "They used a key, and they were carrying one of our chocolate boxes. The special ones, with the festival logo."

I frowned. "Are you sure? The only person who had those was—"

"Abigail," Aunt Nettie finished, her expression troubled.

A chill ran down my spine. The vacant storefront had been empty for months, ever since the antique shop had closed down. As far as I knew, no one had shown serious interest in the space.

"Maybe she's conducting some kind of inspection for her project," I suggested, but the explanation felt thin even to my own ears.

Bunny glanced at the clock. "Shouldn't you two be leaving for the committee meeting soon? It's almost quarter to seven."

Aunt Nettie nodded. "We should stop by the vacant shop on our way. If Abigail's using it as a staging area for her project, we should know what we're up against."

"Good idea," I agreed, grabbing my jacket. "Bunny, are you sure you don't mind closing up alone?"

"I've got this," she assured me, though her nervous smile suggested otherwise. "I'll just finish cleaning up and set the alarm. No problem at all."

"Call if you need anything," I reminded her as Aunt Nettie and I headed for the door. "And Bunny? Thanks for holding down the fort today. You did great."

Her face lit up with genuine pleasure. "Really? Even with the napkin thing?"

"Even with the napkin thing," I confirmed with a smile.

Outside, the early spring evening had turned cool, with a hint of rain in the air. The town square was quiet, most shops already closed for the day. A few restaurants around the perimeter were lighting up for dinner service, warm golden light spilling onto the sidewalks.

"What do you think Abigail was doing in the vacant shop?" Aunt Nettie wondered as we walked toward the storefront adjacent to Heavenly Confections.

"I don't know, but I intend to find out." I tried the door, unsurprised to find it locked. "Do you still have that spare key Mr. Fenton gave you when they were renovating?"

Aunt Nettie raised an eyebrow. "Lee Woodyard, are you suggesting we break in?"

"It's not breaking in if we have a key," I reasoned. "Besides, if Abigail is using this space to plan some kind of takeover of our building, don't we have a right to know?"

She sighed but rummaged in her purse, eventually producing a small key ring. "I've been meaning to return this for months. Mr. Fenton only gave it to me so the workers could use our restroom during the renovation."

"Well, now I'm glad you procrastinated," I said as she unlocked the door.

The interior of the vacant shop was dark and musty, with ghostly shapes of empty display cases and abandoned shelving units looming in the shadows. I fumbled for a light switch, but nothing happened when I flicked it.

"Power's probably off," Aunt Nettie whispered, though there was no real reason to be quiet. "I have a flashlight on my phone."

The beam of light swept across the empty space, revealing dust-covered floors and cobwebbed corners. Nothing seemed out of place or unusual—until the light caught a splash of color near the back of the store.

"What's that?" I moved forward cautiously, Aunt Nettie close behind me.

As we approached, my heart began to pound. Lying on the floor was one of our specialty Easter bunnies, the festival logo clearly visible on its chocolate body. Next to it was a familiar floral scarf—Bunny's scarf—and beyond that. . .

"Oh my God," Aunt Nettie gasped as the flashlight beam illuminated Abigail Thornton's face, her eyes staring sightlessly at the ceiling, a half-eaten chocolate bunny still clutched in her lifeless hand.

I stumbled backward, bumping into my aunt who let out a small cry of shock.

"Is she—" I couldn't bring myself to finish the question.

Aunt Nettie knelt down, checking for a pulse, though the unnatural angle of Abigail's neck made the answer obvious.

"She's gone, Lee," she said quietly, her voice shaking. "Abigail is dead."

The chocolate bunny in Abigail's hand suddenly seemed ominous, its cheerful design a macabre contrast to the grim scene. And Bunny's scarf—what was it doing here?

With trembling fingers, I pulled out my phone to call 911, my mind racing with implications. As the dispatcher's voice came on the line, one thought kept circling in my head: our Easter season had just taken a decidedly deadly turn.

Chapter 2: Melting Alibis

The next few hours passed in a blur of flashing lights, stern questions, and disbelieving stares. Detective James Morrison of the Sweetwater Springs Police Department—a relatively new addition to our small town—took charge of the scene with an efficiency that seemed almost cold under the circumstances.

"Let me get this straight," he said, his dark eyes fixed on me as we sat in the makeshift command center they'd established in the community center across the square. "You and your aunt discovered the body at approximately 6:45 PM, after your employee mentioned seeing Ms. Thornton enter the vacant storefront with a box of your chocolates."

I nodded, clutching the paper cup of lukewarm coffee someone had pressed into my hands. "That's right. We were on our way to the Easter festival committee meeting and decided to check it out."

"And you had a key to this vacant property because...?" His eyebrow arched slightly, a gesture I might have found attractive under different circumstances. Detective Morrison was in his late thirties, with the kind of rugged features that suggested he spent his free time hiking mountain trails rather than watching television.

"The previous tenant gave it to my aunt during their renovation," I explained for what felt like the tenth time. "The workers needed access to our bathroom facilities."

He made another note in his small black notebook. "And you never returned this key."

It wasn't a question, but I answered anyway. "We meant to. It just . . . slipped our minds."

"Convenient," he murmured, the word hanging between us like an accusation.

Aunt Nettie, who had been giving her statement to another officer, joined us then. Her normally rosy cheeks were pale, and she'd aged a decade in the span of an evening.

"Detective, I've told Officer Parker everything I know," she said, her voice steadier than I expected. "May I take my niece home now? It's been a very difficult night."

Morrison studied her for a long moment before nodding. "You're both free to go for now. But don't leave town, and we'll need to speak with you again tomorrow." His gaze returned to me. "Both of you."

"We're not going anywhere," I assured him, rising from the uncomfortable plastic chair. "Heavenly Confections has orders to fill, even in the middle of a. . ." I hesitated, the word "murder" sticking in my throat.

"Investigation," Morrison supplied flatly. "And speaking of your shop, I'll need to interview your employee first thing in the morning. Ms. Birdsong, correct?"

My stomach tightened. "Bunny, yes. But surely you don't think she had anything to do with this?"

"Her scarf was found at the scene, Ms. Woodyard." His tone was matter-of-fact, as if he were discussing the weather rather than implying our employee might be a killer.

"Which means someone is trying to frame her," I countered, feeling a surge of protective anger. "Bunny Birdsong is the least threatening person I've ever met. She apologizes to chocolate molds when she drops them."

A ghost of a smile flickered across Morrison's face before vanishing. "Nevertheless, I'll need to speak with her. 8 AM sharp at the station."

"I'll make sure she's there," I promised, though I had no idea how Bunny would react to the news. She'd gone home before we discovered the body, blissfully unaware of the horror unfolding next door to our shop.

Aunt Nettie slipped her arm through mine. "Come on, Lee. Let's go home."

Outside, the town square had transformed from its usual quaint charm to a scene of morbid curiosity. Yellow police tape cordoned off the vacant storefront, and a small crowd of locals huddled in groups, whispering behind their hands. Several heads turned our way as we emerged, and the whispers intensified.

"Don't look at them," Aunt Nettie advised quietly. "Just keep walking."

We made it halfway across the square before Mayor Wilson intercepted us, his round face flushed with what might have been concern or merely the exertion of hurrying to catch us.

"Nettie, Lee," he puffed, adjusting his ill-fitting sports coat. "What a terrible tragedy. Just terrible. I came as soon as I heard."

"Thank you, Frank," Aunt Nettie replied with the practiced politeness she reserved for town officials. "It's been quite a shock."

"Of course, of course." He dabbed at his forehead with a handkerchief. "The committee meeting's been canceled, naturally. But we'll reschedule once this . . . unpleasantness . . . is behind us."

I stared at him incredulously. "Unpleasantness? Frank, Abigail Thornton is dead. Possibly murdered. And you're worried about rescheduling a meeting about chocolate fountains?"

The mayor had the grace to look abashed. "Now, Lee, I didn't mean it like that. It's just . . . the Easter festival is only two weeks away. We need to keep things moving forward. For the town's sake."

"The town will survive if the Easter Bunny arrives a few days late," I snapped, my patience frayed beyond repair.

Aunt Nettie squeezed my arm in warning. "What Lee means, Frank, is that we're all a bit overwhelmed right now. Perhaps we could discuss festival plans tomorrow, after we've had a chance to process everything?"

The mayor nodded eagerly, relieved to retreat from my glare. "Yes, yes, of course. Tomorrow. We'll touch base tomorrow. You ladies get some rest now."

As he scurried away, I let out a long breath. "Sorry, Aunt Nettie. I know I shouldn't have snapped at him."

"Under the circumstances, I think you showed remarkable restraint," she replied dryly. "Now, let's really go home before someone else tries to discuss centerpieces or bunny-shaped napkin rings."

***

Sleep proved elusive that night. Every time I closed my eyes, I saw Abigail's lifeless form on the dusty floor of the vacant shop, that half-eaten chocolate bunny clutched in her rigid fingers. Around 3 AM, I gave up and went downstairs to the kitchen of the cozy Victorian house I shared with Aunt Nettie.

To my surprise, the light was already on, and the kettle was whistling softly on the stove. Aunt Nettie looked up from where she sat at the kitchen table, a steaming mug of tea in front of her.

"I thought I might have company," she said, getting up to fetch another mug from the cabinet. "Chamomile or peppermint?"

"Chamomile," I decided, sinking into a chair. "I can't stop thinking about it, Aunt Nettie. Who would want to kill Abigail?"

She set a mug of tea in front of me, the gentle fragrance of chamomile rising with the steam. "The more pertinent question might be, who wouldn't? Abigail Thornton wasn't exactly beloved in this town."

I wrapped my hands around the warm mug. "But to actually murder her? That's a big leap from disliking someone."

"People have killed for less," Aunt Nettie observed, resuming her seat. "And Abigail had her fingers in a lot of pies—not just our chocolate ones. That development project of hers would have affected half the businesses in town."

I nodded slowly. "She came to the shop specifically to tell us about it. Almost like she was . . . gloating."

"That was Abigail's way. She enjoyed wielding power." Aunt Nettie took a thoughtful sip of her tea. "But there's something that doesn't add up about all this."

"The chocolate bunny," I said immediately. "Why would she be eating one of our specialty bunnies in an empty shop? And how did Bunny's scarf end up there?"

Aunt Nettie's expression grew troubled. "That's what worries me, Lee. It looks very bad for Bunny."

"You don't actually believe she had anything to do with this?" I set my mug down with more force than necessary, tea sloshing over the rim.

"Of course not," she soothed. "But the evidence . . . it's rather damning."

I wiped up the spilled tea with a napkin, my mind racing. "We need to talk to Bunny first thing tomorrow. Before she goes to the police station."

"To make sure she gets her story straight?" Aunt Nettie raised an eyebrow.

"To make sure she doesn't incriminate herself out of sheer nervousness," I corrected. "You know how she gets when she's flustered. She could confess to assassinating JFK if someone stared at her hard enough."

Aunt Nettie couldn't suppress a small smile. "You're right about that. Poor girl tends to babble when she's anxious." Her smile faded. "But Lee, we need to be careful. If Detective Morrison thinks we're interfering with his investigation. . ."

"We're not interfering," I insisted. "We're just looking out for our employee. And anyway, no one knows Sweetwater Springs like we do. The police might miss something important."

"Like what?"

I shrugged, frustrated. "I don't know yet. But there's more going on here than just Abigail's development project. Bunny mentioned that her ex-husband had some kind of business arrangement with Abigail. And he came to warn her about something today."

"Beau Birdsong," Aunt Nettie mused. "I never did like that man. Too slick by half, just like his father."

"We should talk to him too," I decided, warming to the idea of conducting our own parallel investigation. "Find out what this mysterious arrangement was."

Aunt Nettie eyed me over the rim of her mug. "Lee Woodyard, are you suggesting we play detective?"

"I'm suggesting we protect our business and our employee," I replied, though she wasn't entirely wrong. "If Bunny gets arrested because of circumstantial evidence, it doesn't just affect her—it affects Heavenly Confections too. Who's going to buy chocolate from a shop where the employee is suspected of murder?"

"You make a valid point," she conceded. "But promise me you'll be careful. Whoever killed Abigail is still out there."

I reached across the table and squeezed her hand. "I promise. Now, try to get some sleep. Tomorrow's going to be a long day."

***

By 7 AM, I was already on my third cup of coffee and pacing the kitchen when my phone rang. The caller ID showed Bunny's name, and I nearly knocked over a chair in my haste to answer.

"Bunny? Are you okay?"

Her voice came through high and breathless. "Lee! Oh my goodness, I just heard about Ms. Thornton! It's all over town! They're saying she was murdered with one of our chocolate bunnies! Is it true? Please tell me it's not true!"

I winced, holding the phone away from my ear slightly. "Bunny, calm down. Where are you right now?"

"Home. Well, not my real home—that's still with Beau, technically, until the divorce is final—but the little apartment above the bookstore that I'm renting from Mrs. Henderson. She woke me up to tell me about Ms. Thornton, and then she gave me this really strange look, like she thought I might have done it, which is ridiculous because I would never—"

"Bunny," I interrupted firmly. "I need you to take a deep breath. Can you do that for me?"

I heard her inhale shakily. "Okay. Breathing."

"Good. Now listen carefully. The police want to talk to you this morning. They've asked you to come to the station at 8 AM."

There was a moment of stunned silence, then a small, terrified squeak. "The police? Why me? Oh no, is it because of my scarf? I noticed it was missing last night when I got home, but I just thought I'd left it at the shop or maybe dropped it somewhere, I'm always losing things, but I never thought—"

"Bunny," I cut in again, "I'm going to pick you up in fifteen minutes. Don't talk to anyone else before then, okay? And especially don't talk to any reporters if they call or show up at your door."

"Reporters?" Her voice rose an octave. "Why would reporters care about me?"

I silently cursed myself for making her more anxious. "They probably won't. I'm just saying, as a precaution. Fifteen minutes, okay?"

"Okay," she agreed meekly. "Should I wear something specific? I don't know what the dress code is for police questioning. Is black too formal? Too funeral? Maybe pastels would seem too cheerful under the circumstances—"

"Whatever you're comfortable in is fine," I assured her, making a mental note to get there in ten minutes rather than fifteen. "See you soon."

I ended the call and turned to find Aunt Nettie watching me from the doorway, already dressed in one of her practical pantsuits.

"I'm going to the shop to assess the damage," she announced.

"Damage?" I echoed, confused. "Did something happen to Heavenly Confections?"

"Not physical damage," she clarified. "But you can bet our reputation has taken a hit. Nothing scares off customers like a murder investigation. I need to call our suppliers, talk to our regulars, and generally do damage control."

I nodded, impressed by her practicality. "Good thinking. I'll take Bunny to the police station and then join you at the shop afterward."

"Actually," Aunt Nettie said thoughtfully, "I think you should stick with Bunny for as long as they'll let you. That girl needs an advocate, and you've always been good at standing up for the underdog."

"What about the shop?"

She waved away my concern. "I ran Heavenly Confections for years before you came back to Sweetwater Springs, remember? I can handle a few Easter orders on my own." A wry smile crossed her face. "Besides, playing detective will keep you out of trouble. You get fidgety when you're worried."

I couldn't argue with that assessment. "Alright, I'll stay with Bunny. But call me if you need anything."

"Just one thing before you go," Aunt Nettie's expression grew serious. "Be careful what you say to Detective Morrison. He seems . . . thorough."

"Is that a polite way of saying he suspects us?" I asked, half-joking.

She didn't smile. "It's a polite way of saying he strikes me as the type who sees suspects everywhere. And technically, we did have motive and opportunity."

A chill ran through me as I realized she was right. Abigail had threatened our business just hours before her death, and we had discovered her body in a place few people had access to. From an outsider's perspective, we might look just as suspicious as Bunny.

"I'll watch what I say," I promised, grabbing my purse and car keys. "And Aunt Nettie? You be careful too."

***

I found Bunny pacing in front of the bookstore, wearing a floral dress that seemed aggressively cheerful under the circumstances and clutching a large tote bag to her chest like a shield. Her platinum blonde hair stood up in anxious tufts, as if she'd been running her hands through it repeatedly.

"I tried to look normal," she blurted as she scrambled into my car. "But I don't know what normal looks like when you're being questioned about a murder. Is this okay? It's not too bright, is it? I could go change—"

"The dress is fine," I assured her, pulling away from the curb. "But Bunny, before we get to the station, I need to know exactly what happened yesterday after Aunt Nettie and I left the shop."

Her eyes widened. "You think I had something to do with Ms. Thornton's death?"

"No!" I said quickly. "Of course not. But the police might, especially since. . ." I hesitated, unsure how to break the news about her scarf.

"Since my scarf was found with her body," Bunny finished quietly.

I glanced at her in surprise. "You knew about that?"

She nodded miserably. "Mrs. Henderson told me. She said everyone's talking about it. "That flighty Birdsong girl left her signature scarf at the scene of the crime," she quoted with surprising accuracy. 'Careless of her, but what can you expect from someone who can't even keep a husband?' "

I winced at the typical small-town cruelty. "Mrs. Henderson should mind her own business. And for the record, I think you're better off without Beau."

A ghost of a smile flickered across Bunny's face before disappearing. "Thanks, Lee. But it doesn't change the fact that my scarf was there. And I can't explain how it got there, which makes me look really guilty."

"Let's start with what you do know," I suggested, turning onto Main Street. The police station was only a few blocks from the town square. "After we left, what happened at the shop?"

Bunny twisted her hands in her lap. "Nothing unusual. A couple more customers came in. I filled their orders, cleaned up, and closed the shop around 7:30."

"Did you leave the shop at any point? Even for a minute?"

She thought for a moment. "I stepped outside once to take the trash to the dumpster in the back alley. That's usually your job, but I wanted to be helpful."

I nodded encouragingly. "Good. What time was that?"

"Around 7:15, I think? It was starting to get dark."

"And did you see or hear anything unusual while you were out there?"

Bunny's brow furrowed in concentration. "The back door of the vacant shop was open a crack. I remember thinking it was strange, but I figured maybe the realtor had been showing the space earlier."

My pulse quickened. "Did you look inside or go near it?"

"No!" she exclaimed. "Why would I? Empty buildings are creepy."

I felt a mixture of relief and disappointment. Relief that Bunny hadn't potentially contaminated the crime scene, but disappointment that she hadn't seen anything useful.

"What about your scarf? When did you last remember having it?"

She bit her lip. "That's the thing—I'm sure I was wearing it all day. I always wear a scarf; they're kind of my signature accessory.

But when I got home, it was gone." Her eyes suddenly widened. "Wait! I did take it off once, when I was cleaning the kitchen. I remember hanging it on the hook by the back door because I didn't want to get chocolate on it."

"And you didn't put it back on when you took out the trash?" I pressed, seeing a possible explanation.

Bunny shook her head emphatically. "No, I got distracted by a text from my sister and completely forgot about it. But that means. . ." Her face paled as the implication sank in. "Someone must have gone into the shop and taken it."

Or you went next door and dropped it, a small, unwelcome voice whispered in the back of my mind. I pushed the thought away immediately. "The back door was locked when you left, right?"

"Of course! I double-checked everything. The alarm was set, all doors were locked." Bunny's eyes filled with tears. "Lee, you believe me, don't you? I would never hurt anyone, especially not with chocolate. That would be . . . sacrilegious."

Despite the seriousness of the situation, I had to smile at her choice of words. "I believe you, Bunny. And we're going to make sure Detective Morrison believes you too."

We had reached the police station, a modest brick building that seemed too small to house a murder investigation. I parked in the visitor's lot and turned to face Bunny.

"Just tell the truth, answer only what they ask, and try not to ramble," I advised. "I'll be with you as long as they allow."

She nodded, clutching her tote bag even tighter. "I brought my daily planner as an alibi, but I'm not sure it helps much since I was alone in the shop."

"Every little bit helps," I assured her, though I wasn't convinced a planner would sway Morrison. "Ready?"

"No," she admitted with a shaky laugh. "But let's go anyway."

***

Detective Morrison was waiting for us in a small interview room, a cup of coffee and a manila folder on the table in front of him. His dark eyes assessed Bunny coolly as she perched on the edge of a chair, her tote bag still clutched to her chest.

"Ms. Birdsong," he nodded in greeting, then turned to me. "Ms. Woodyard, I don't recall inviting you to this interview."

"I'm here as moral support," I replied firmly. "Bunny is understandably upset."

"This is an official police interview, not a tea party," he pointed out, though he didn't explicitly tell me to leave. "But you can stay for now, as long as you don't interfere."

I took the chair next to Bunny, who shot me a grateful look.

Morrison opened the folder and removed several photographs, which he arranged in front of Bunny. I realized with a jolt that they were crime scene photos—including close-ups of Abigail's body and the half-eaten chocolate bunny in her hand.

"Do you recognize this woman, Ms. Birdsong?" Morrison asked, his voice deceptively casual.

Bunny swallowed hard, her gaze skittering around the edges of the photos. "That's Ms. Thornton. Abigail Thornton."

"And did you have a relationship with Ms. Thornton?"

"Not really," Bunny replied, her voice small. "I mean, I knew who she was—everyone in town does—but we weren't friends or anything."

Morrison made a note. "Yet witnesses say they observed you having what appeared to be a heated conversation with Ms. Thornton outside Thompson's Grocery last week. Would you care to explain that?"

Bunny's eyes widened. "It wasn't heated! Well, not on my side, anyway. She was upset with me, but I was just trying to get to my car."

"What was she upset about?"

"My divorce," Bunny explained, twisting her hands nervously. "She and my husband—soon-to-be ex-husband—have some kind of business arrangement. She blamed me for causing problems with it."

Morrison leaned forward slightly. "What kind of business arrangement?"

"I don't know exactly," Bunny admitted. "Beau never discussed his business with me. He said I wouldn't understand it anyway."

I bristled at the casual sexism, but kept quiet, reminding myself I was here as moral support, not an interrogator.

"Let's move on to yesterday," Morrison continued smoothly. "You were working at Heavenly Confections all day?"

Bunny nodded eagerly. "Yes, from 7:30 AM until closing at 7:30 PM. Well, actually I stayed until about 7:45 to clean up and set the alarm."

"And during that time, did you have any contact with Ms. Thornton?"

"She came into the shop in the afternoon," Bunny recalled. "She spoke mostly with Lee and Ms. Woodyard—I mean, the other Ms. Woodyard, Lee's aunt." She flushed, realizing she was starting to ramble. "I didn't really talk to her."

Morrison's gaze flicked to me briefly before returning to Bunny. "After Ms. Woodyard and her aunt left the shop, did you leave at any point?"

"Just to take out the trash around 7:15," Bunny replied. "But I came right back in."

"Did you go anywhere near the vacant storefront next door?"

"No," she said firmly. "The only time I was outside was to go to the dumpster in the back alley."

Morrison nodded, then picked up another photo from the folder. This one showed Bunny's floral scarf, laid out on what appeared to be an evidence table.

"Do you recognize this, Ms. Birdsong?"

Bunny nodded miserably. "It's my scarf. I was wearing it yesterday."

"When did you last remember having it?"

"I took it off when I was cleaning the kitchen at the shop," she explained, just as she had to me in the car. "I hung it on the hook by the back door. But when I got home, I realized I didn't have it anymore."

"So you're saying you left it at the shop?" Morrison's tone was skeptical.

"Yes! I must have forgotten to put it back on after cleaning."

"Yet it was found next to Abigail Thornton's body in the vacant storefront," he pointed out. "Can you explain how it got there?"

Tears welled in Bunny's eyes. "No, I can't. Someone must have taken it from the shop."

"Or," Morrison suggested, his voice hardening slightly, "you went next door, had an altercation with Ms. Thornton, and left your scarf behind in your haste to escape the scene."

"I didn't!" Bunny protested, a tear spilling down her cheek. "I never left the shop except to take out the trash! And I would never hurt anyone, especially not with chocolate!"

I couldn't stay silent any longer. "Detective, surely you don't think Bunny capable of murder. She's been working at Heavenly

Confections for less than a month. Why would she kill Abigail Thornton?"

Morrison turned his cool gaze on me. "Perhaps because her ex-husband had a business arrangement with the victim? An arrangement that might have affected her divorce settlement?"

I blinked, surprised by the suggestion. I hadn't considered that angle.

"That's not it at all!" Bunny exclaimed. "I don't care about Beau's money. I just want out of the marriage." She swallowed hard. "You can ask my lawyer if you don't believe me. I've turned down every settlement offer because they all come with conditions—like keeping quiet about certain things."

That piqued my interest. "What things, Bunny?"

She shook her head, looking truly frightened for the first time. "I can't. . . Beau said if I ever told anyone, he'd make sure I had nothing. Not even my name."

Morrison's eyebrow arched. "That sounds like a threat, Ms. Birdsong. Did you report it?"

"To who?" she asked with surprising bitterness. "Beau's family practically owns this town. His father plays golf with the judge who's handling our divorce."

I felt a surge of sympathy and renewed protectiveness. Whatever was going on between Bunny and her ex, it clearly went deeper than a simple divorce.

Morrison seemed to sense it too. He studied Bunny for a long moment, then closed the folder. "I think that's enough for now, Ms. Birdsong. You're free to go, but don't leave town. We'll be in touch if we have more questions."

Bunny sagged with relief. "So I'm not under arrest?"

"Not at this time," Morrison replied, which wasn't exactly the reassurance she was looking for.

As we stood to leave, he added, "One more thing, Ms. Birdsong. The chocolate bunny found in Ms. Thornton's hand—it was poisoned. Specifically, it contained a concentrated dose of peanut oil, which triggered a severe allergic reaction. Ms. Thornton was known to have a life-threatening peanut allergy."

Bunny gasped. "That's terrible! But all of our Easter festival bunnies were made with special care to be nut-free. Ms. Woodyard—I mean, Lee's aunt—was very strict about it because of Ms. Thornton's allergy."

Morrison's gaze sharpened. "So you knew about her allergy?"

"Everyone knew," I interjected quickly. "Abigail made sure of it. She wore a medical alert bracelet and carried an EpiPen. And Aunt Nettie insisted on making all the festival chocolates in a completely nut-free environment."

The detective made another note. "Interesting that the murderer chose a method so specifically tailored to the victim, isn't it? Almost as if they had insider knowledge of both her allergy and your chocolate-making process."

The implication hung in the air between us, and I felt a chill run down my spine. Morrison wasn't just suspicious of Bunny—he was keeping an eye on all of us at Heavenly Confections.

"Is that all, Detective?" I asked, keeping my voice steady despite my racing heart.

He nodded once. "For now. Good day, ladies."

Outside the police station, Bunny practically collapsed against my car, her legs seemingly unable to support her anymore.

"That was horrible," she whispered, wiping away tears. "He thinks I did it, doesn't he? He thinks I poisoned her with chocolate."

I squeezed her shoulder reassuringly. "He's just doing his job, looking at all possibilities. But something doesn't add up, Bunny. If you took your scarf off in the shop and someone planted it at the crime scene, they must have been trying to frame you specifically."

Her eyes widened. "Why would anyone do that?"

"I don't know," I admitted. "But I intend to find out." I opened the car door for her. "Come on, let's get to the shop. Aunt Nettie is handling everything alone, and with Easter coming up, we need all hands on deck."

As I started the car, Bunny turned to me with a mixture of gratitude and anxiety. "Lee? Thank you for believing me. But . . . what if no one else does? What if they arrest me?"

I gripped the steering wheel tightly, determination growing. "They won't. Because we're going to find out who really killed Abigail Thornton."

"We?" she echoed, sounding both hopeful and terrified.

"Yes, we," I confirmed, pulling out of the parking lot. "Aunt Nettie and I don't just make the best chocolate in three counties—we're also pretty good at solving puzzles. And right now, there's a deadly puzzle that needs solving before someone else gets hurt."

Or before our Easter season is completely ruined, I added silently. Because as much as I wanted justice for Abigail, I also needed to protect Heavenly Confections. Without the Easter rush, our small business might not survive to see another holiday season.

As we drove toward the town square, I couldn't help noticing the curious stares from pedestrians as they recognized my car. News traveled fast in Sweetwater Springs, and by now, everyone would know about our connection to the murder. I only hoped our chocolate's reputation was strong enough to withstand the whispers.

One thing was certain: this Easter was shaping up to be anything but sweet.

Chapter 3: Bitter Truths

By the time Bunny and I reached Heavenly Confections, I half expected to find the shop deserted—the chocolate murder making potential customers wary of our treats. Instead, I was shocked to discover a line stretching from our door halfway down the block.

"What on earth?" I murmured as I parked around back.

Bunny peered through the windshield, equally confused. "Is there a sale I don't know about?"

We hurried through the back entrance into the kitchen, where we found Aunt Nettie furiously tempering chocolate, a fine sheen of sweat on her forehead despite the carefully controlled temperature of the room.

"Thank goodness you're here," she greeted us without looking up from her work. "We're absolutely swamped."

"We noticed," I said, quickly tying on an apron. "What's going on? I thought the murder would keep people away, not draw them in."

Aunt Nettie shook her head, a wry smile playing at her lips. "Never underestimate the appeal of notoriety, my dear. Everyone in town wants to see the shop where 'murder chocolate' was made."

"That's horrible!" Bunny exclaimed, her hand flying to her mouth.

"That's human nature," Aunt Nettie corrected. "Morbid curiosity is a powerful force. The good news is, they're buying chocolate almost as fast as I can make it."

I frowned, not sure how I felt about profiting from Abigail's death. "Shouldn't we close for a day out of respect?"

Aunt Nettie finally looked up, fixing me with a steady gaze. "And give credence to the rumors that our shop was somehow responsible? No, Lee. The best thing we can do right now is carry on normally. Show the town that Heavenly Confections has nothing to hide."

She had a point. Besides, we needed the business, especially with Easter so close.

"Bunny, can you handle the register?" I asked, already pulling out ingredients for a fresh batch of chocolate eggs. "And try not to answer any questions about Abigail or the investigation."

She nodded, though she looked terrified at the prospect of facing the curious crowd. "What should I say if people ask?"

"Just tell them it's an ongoing police matter and you're not at liberty to discuss it," Aunt Nettie advised. "Then offer them a sample of our new raspberry truffles. That should change the subject."

As Bunny headed to the front, I turned to my aunt. "How did it go with Detective Morrison? He seems to think Bunny had a motive because of some business deal between Abigail and Beau."

Aunt Nettie's hands stilled momentarily. "He pressed me pretty hard about that. Asked if I knew what kind of arrangement they had."

"And do you?" I asked, surprised.

She shrugged lightly. "This town has no secrets, only varying degrees of public knowledge. I've heard rumors that Beau and Abigail were partnering on some real estate ventures. Properties ripe for development once her restoration project went through."

"Like our building?" I suggested, understanding dawning. "That's why she was so confident Mr. Jenkins would sell to her—because Beau's family has connections to everyone in town."

"It's possible," Aunt Nettie agreed. "Though why Bunny would kill her over that is beyond me. If anything, Abigail's death might complicate her divorce further."

I repeated what Bunny had told Morrison about refusing settlement offers because they came with conditions about keeping quiet. "She said Beau threatened that she'd have nothing, not even her name, if she talked about 'certain things.'"

Aunt Nettie's eyebrows rose. "Now that is interesting. What things, I wonder?"

"I don't know, but I intend to find out." I lowered my voice, though the noise from the busy shop front would have covered our conversation. "Bunny mentioned that Beau came by the shop yesterday looking for her. Said he wanted to warn her about something. What if he knew Abigail was in danger?"

"Or what if he was setting Bunny up?" Aunt Nettie countered. "The timing is certainly suspicious."

I hadn't considered that angle, but it made a terrible kind of sense. If Beau had planned to kill Abigail, warning Bunny beforehand could establish an alibi for himself while simultaneously directing suspicion toward her.

"We need to talk to him," I decided. "Find out what this warning was about."

"Be careful, Lee," Aunt Nettie cautioned. "The Birdsong family isn't known for taking kindly to people who meddle in their affairs."

"I'm not meddling," I protested. "I'm investigating. There's a difference."

"Not to them, there isn't." She sighed, returning to her chocolate work. "Just promise me you won't confront Beau alone. Take me or, better yet, talk to him somewhere public."

Before I could respond, the kitchen door swung open and Bunny poked her head in, looking frazzled. "Lee? There's someone here asking for you specifically. Says it's urgent."

"Who is it?"

"Beau," she replied, her voice barely above a whisper. "My Beau. I mean, not my Beau anymore, but—you know what I mean."

I exchanged a significant look with Aunt Nettie. "Perfect timing. Tell him I'll be right out."

After Bunny retreated, Aunt Nettie grasped my arm. "Remember what I said. Public place."

"We'll be in a shop full of people," I reminded her. "It doesn't get more public than that."

She didn't look entirely convinced but released me with a nod. "Just listen more than you talk. Beau Birdsong has a silver tongue, just like his father."

I gave her a quick, reassuring smile before heading out to the main shop floor. The place was indeed packed, with Bunny efficiently ringing up purchases while fielding what I assumed were thinly veiled questions about the murder. She was handling it better than I expected, her natural cheerfulness providing a buffer against the more morbid inquiries.

Beau Birdsong stood near the display of Easter baskets, looking as out of place in our quaint chocolate shop as a wolf in a rabbit hutch. Tall and lean, with the kind of rugged good looks that graced men's fashion magazines, he exuded the casual confidence of someone who'd never heard the word "no" in his life. His tailored suit probably cost more than our monthly rent, and his expertly styled hair hadn't dared to move in the spring breeze.

"Mr. Birdsong," I greeted him coolly. "Bunny says you wanted to see me."

His smile was practiced and perfect. "Ms. Woodyard. Thank you for making time. I know you must be . . . overwhelmed . . . given recent events."

The way he emphasized "overwhelmed" made it sound like an accusation rather than an expression of sympathy.

"We're managing," I replied. "Though I'm curious why you'd want to speak with me rather than your wife."

"Soon-to-be ex-wife," he corrected smoothly. "And I tried to speak with Bunny yesterday, but the timing wasn't right." His gaze drifted to where Bunny was carefully avoiding looking in our direction. "She seems busy today as well."

"We all are," I pointed out. "What can I help you with?"

Beau's smile tightened fractionally. "Perhaps we could speak somewhere more private? This isn't exactly a conversation for public consumption."

I remembered Aunt Nettie's warning and stood my ground. "I'm afraid that's not possible right now. Whatever you have to say will have to be said here."

He studied me for a moment, as if recalculating his approach. "Very well. I came to discuss Abigail Thornton."

"What about her?"

"I understand you found the body." It wasn't a question, but I nodded anyway. "Then you're aware of how she died."

"Poisoned chocolate," I confirmed, keeping my voice low despite the noise in the shop. "A specialty Easter bunny from our shop."

Beau's expression remained unreadable. "That's unfortunate for your business."

"Especially since someone seems to be trying to frame Bunny for the murder," I added, watching his reaction carefully.

If I expected a dramatic response, I was disappointed. Beau merely raised an eyebrow. "Is that what you think happened?"

"Her scarf was found at the scene," I pointed out. "A scarf she left hanging in our shop. Someone took it deliberately to implicate her."

"Or she dropped it herself," he countered. "Bunny has always been . . . careless with her possessions."

The subtle dig made my jaw clench. "Why are you here, Mr. Birdsong? If you're concerned about your wife—"

"Ex-wife," he interjected again.

"—then perhaps you should be at the police station vouching for her character, not in my shop implying her guilt."

For the first time, a flash of genuine emotion crossed his face—something like anger, quickly masked. "I'm not implying anything, Ms. Woodyard. I'm simply here to offer some advice."

"Which is?"

He leaned in slightly, his voice dropping to a near whisper. "Stay out of matters that don't concern you. Abigail's death is unfortunate, but it's a police matter now. Your amateur sleuthing will only complicate things."

I blinked, taken aback. "I don't know what you're talking about."

"Don't you?" His smile returned, cold and knowing. "The town talks, Ms. Woodyard. I know you and your aunt have a reputation for poking your noses into things. This time, I strongly suggest you resist the urge."

"Is that a threat?" I asked, keeping my voice steady despite the anger bubbling up inside me.

"A friendly warning," he clarified. "Abigail was involved in sensitive business matters that are better left undisturbed. For everyone's sake."

"Including yours?" I challenged.

Before he could respond, a customer accidentally bumped into him, causing him to step back. The moment of tension broken, Beau straightened his already immaculate suit jacket.

"I should be going," he said, his public persona firmly back in place. "Please give my regards to your aunt. And to Bunny, of course."

As he turned to leave, I called after him, "You came to the shop yesterday looking for Bunny. You said you wanted to warn her about something. What was it?"

He paused, looking back at me with an expression I couldn't quite read. "Did I? How interesting." With that cryptic response, he strode out of the shop, the bell jingling cheerfully in his wake.

I stood there for a moment, processing the strange encounter. Far from clarifying anything, Beau's visit had only deepened the mystery. What were these "sensitive business matters" he'd referred to? And why had he gone from wanting to warn Bunny to telling me to stay out of it?

The sound of a throat clearing pulled me from my thoughts. I turned to find Mrs. Peabody, one of our most loyal (and nosiest) customers, standing entirely too close for comfort.

"Such a handsome man," she observed, her eyes still on the door Beau had exited through. "But troubled, I think. His father was the same way—charming on the outside, calculating on the inside."

I managed a polite smile. "Did you need help with something, Mrs. Peabody?"

"Oh, I was just wondering if you'd heard about poor Abigail's list," she replied, her expression shifting to one of exaggerated sympathy that didn't reach her eyes.

"List?" I echoed.

Mrs. Peabody nodded eagerly, leaning in as if to share a great secret. "They say the police found a list in her personal effects. Names of people in town—people who had crossed her or owed her in some way." She lowered her voice further. "Margaret Wilkins says her name was on it. And the mayor's too."

I fought to keep my expression neutral. "I'm sure the police are exploring all angles, Mrs. Peabody."

"Mmm, yes," she agreed, though she looked disappointed by my measured response. "Well, I should get in line. Those Easter cream eggs sell out so quickly."

As she wandered away, I made a mental note to add "Abigail's list" to my growing collection of clues. If such a list really existed, it could point to other potential suspects—people who had motives to want Abigail dead that had nothing to do with Heavenly Confections or Bunny.

The morning rush continued unabated, keeping all three of us too busy for further discussion until nearly lunchtime, when the crowd finally thinned enough for Aunt Nettie to flip the "Open" sign to "Closed for Lunch."

"One hour," she announced, rubbing her lower back as the last customer departed. "I need to sit down and you two need to fill me in on everything."

In the kitchen, as we munched on sandwiches Aunt Nettie had prepared before our arrival, I recounted my conversation with Beau.

"So he came here specifically to warn you off investigating?" Aunt Nettie looked troubled. "That's rather bold."

"And suspicious," I added. "Why would he care if we looked into Abigail's death unless he had something to hide?"

Bunny, who had been uncharacteristically quiet, finally spoke up. "Beau always has something to hide. That's just who he is." She picked at the crust of her sandwich. "When we were married, there were whole areas of his life I wasn't allowed to ask about. His business dealings, certain friends, phone calls that would end abruptly when I entered the room. . ."

"Did you ever see him with Abigail?" I asked gently.

She nodded. "A few times. They always claimed it was about community development projects, but. . ." She hesitated.

"But?" Aunt Nettie prompted.

"There was something off about it," Bunny continued reluctantly. "The way they'd stop talking when I approached. And once, I overheard Abigail telling him, 'Remember our agreement. Fifty-fifty, no matter what they offer.'"

I exchanged a look with Aunt Nettie. "That sounds like more than community development."

"It could have been about anything," Bunny said with a sigh. "That's the problem with Beau. Everything is vague and deniable.

That's why I finally left him. Living with someone you can never fully trust is just. . ." She trailed off, her eyes downcast.

"Exhausting," Aunt Nettie supplied. "And unhealthy."

Bunny nodded gratefully. "Exactly. But even though I left, I still feel like I'm caught in his web somehow. And now with Abigail's murder and my scarf at the scene. . ." Her voice trembled slightly.

An idea was forming in my mind, one I wasn't sure I should voice. But looking at Bunny's worried face, I decided honesty was the best approach.

"Bunny, I need to ask you something, and I want you to really think before you answer," I said carefully. "Is it possible that Beau is setting you up to take the fall for Abigail's murder?"

Her eyes widened. "You mean . . . deliberately framing me?"

"It would explain a lot," I pointed out. "He knew about your scarf in the shop. He came by yesterday, possibly to establish an alibi for himself while making you look suspicious. And today he practically warned me against investigating further."

"But why would he kill Abigail?" Bunny asked, bewildered. "They were business partners or something."

"Maybe their partnership went sour," Aunt Nettie suggested. "Or maybe he wanted to silence her before she could reveal something damaging about him."

Bunny considered this for a long moment, her normally expressive face unusually still. "It's possible," she finally admitted. "Beau can be . . . ruthless when he feels threatened. And lately, he's been acting strange—anxious, almost. The divorce negotiations have been getting increasingly hostile."

"Speaking of which," I remembered Mrs. Peabody's gossip, "have you heard anything about a list that Abigail supposedly kept? Names of people who had crossed her or owed her favors?"

Bunny shook her head, but Aunt Nettie's expression turned thoughtful.

"I've heard whispers," she admitted. "Abigail had a talent for discovering people's secrets and using them to her advantage. It wouldn't surprise me if she kept records."

"If such a list exists, we need to see it," I declared. "The more potential suspects we can identify, the better chance we have of shifting suspicion away from Bunny."

"And how exactly do you propose we get access to police evidence?" Aunt Nettie asked dryly.

I smiled. "We don't need the original. We just need to know who was on it. And for that, we need to talk to someone who's already seen it or heard about its contents."

"Margaret Wilkins," Aunt Nettie said immediately, catching my train of thought. "Mrs. Peabody mentioned she knew her name was on the list."

"Exactly. And as head of the gardening club and Abigail's rival for the Easter festival chairmanship, she might have insights beyond just the list."

Bunny looked back and forth between us, a mixture of hope and anxiety on her face. "Do you really think you can clear my name?"

"We can certainly try," I assured her, though I knew it wouldn't be easy. "But we need to be smart about this. Detective Morrison is already watching us closely."

Aunt Nettie checked her watch. "Margaret usually tends to the community garden beds in the town square during lunch hours. If you hurry, you might catch her there."

I nodded, quickly finishing my sandwich and standing. "Perfect. I'll say I'm checking on the garden bed near our outdoor seating area for the Easter festival."

"What should I do?" Bunny asked, eager to help.

"Stay here with Aunt Nettie," I advised. "The less attention you draw to yourself right now, the better. And maybe try calling your divorce lawyer. See if they know anything about Beau and Abigail's business dealings."

As I headed for the door, Aunt Nettie called after me, "Remember, Lee—observe and inquire, don't accuse. Margaret has a prickly temperament and a long memory for slights."

"I'll be the soul of tact," I promised, grabbing a light jacket for the mild spring day.

Outside, the town square was quieter than earlier, with most people taking their lunch breaks indoors. A gentle breeze carried the scent of blooming flowers and freshly turned soil—a reminder that despite murder and intrigue, the natural world continued its cycle of renewal.

Sure enough, Margaret Wilkins was kneeling beside one of the square's elaborate garden beds, her gray hair tucked under a wide-brimmed hat, gardening gloves covered in soil. At seventy-two, she moved with the vigor of someone decades younger, carefully pruning and shaping the early spring plantings.

"Good afternoon, Mrs. Wilkins," I greeted her cheerfully. "The beds are looking beautiful already."

She glanced up, her sharp eyes assessing me over the rim of her bifocals. "Lee Woodyard. I wondered when you'd come seeking me out." She returned to her pruning without waiting for my response.

I blinked, thrown off-balance by her direct approach. "I'm sorry?"

"Oh, don't play coy," she scoffed, though not unkindly. "Your aunt Nettie probably told you I'm out here during lunch hours. And given what's happened, it was only a matter of time before you started asking questions around town." She sat back on her heels, fixing me with a penetrating stare. "You Woodyard women have a reputation for curiosity, you know."

I couldn't help but smile at her frankness. "Is that a polite way of saying we're nosy?"

"If the shoe fits," she replied with a hint of a smile. "Though in this case, I suppose your nosiness is understandable. Murdered customers are bad for business."

"It's more than that," I said, dropping the pretense. "Bunny Birdsong is being set up to take the fall, and I intend to find out who's really responsible."

Margaret removed her gardening gloves and patted the bench beside her. "Sit, child. No point in looming over me like the shadow of doom."

I complied, settling onto the bench as she joined me, her movements surprisingly fluid for a woman her age.

"You think Bunny is innocent," she stated rather than asked.

"I know she is," I replied firmly. "Bunny might be clumsy and a bit scattered, but she's not a killer. And she certainly wouldn't use chocolate as a murder weapon."

Margaret's lips twitched. "No, I suppose that would be rather sacrilegious for someone in her profession." She studied me thoughtfully. "What do you want from me, Lee?"

"Information," I admitted. "I heard there was a list found among Abigail's things. A list of names—people she had some kind of hold over. And I heard your name was on it."

Her expression tightened, but she didn't deny it. "News travels fast in this town."

"Then it's true?"

Margaret sighed heavily, suddenly looking her age. "Yes, it's true. Though how anyone knows about that list already is beyond me. The police only interviewed me this morning."

"What did they ask you?"

"The usual. Where was I yesterday evening, did I have any conflicts with Abigail—which I most certainly did—and what did I know about her list."

I leaned forward slightly. "And what did you tell them?"

"The truth," she replied simply. "That Abigail Thornton was a manipulative, power-hungry woman who used people's secrets and mistakes against them to get what she wanted."

"Including yours?" I asked carefully.

Margaret's gaze drifted to the garden beds, their carefully arranged flowers just beginning to show their spring colors. "Twenty years ago, I had an affair with a married man. It ended badly, and I've regretted it ever since. Somehow, Abigail discovered letters we'd exchanged—letters I thought had been destroyed."

"And she blackmailed you with them?"

"Not for money," Margaret clarified. "For influence. Votes on the town council, support for her projects, stepping down from committees when she wanted to take over." Her mouth twisted bitterly. "The Easter festival chairmanship was just the latest example. I've run that festival for fifteen years, but this year, Abigail decided she wanted it. One hint that those letters might find their way to the historical society's archives, and suddenly I was 'volunteering' to let her take the reins."

"That's awful," I said, genuinely sympathetic despite the fact that Margaret had just supplied herself with a pretty solid motive for murder.

As if reading my thoughts, she snorted. "Yes, I had reason to want her gone. So did half the town. But before you start wondering if I poisoned a chocolate bunny with exotic plant toxins from my garden, let me save you the trouble. I was at the senior center last night from six until eight, teaching a gardening workshop to at least twenty witnesses."

"I wasn't accusing you," I protested.

"Of course you were, dear," she said without rancor. "And you'd be a fool not to. But while I'm not sorry Abigail is dead, I didn't kill her."

I believed her, oddly enough. Whether it was her forthright manner or the genuine bitterness in her voice when she spoke of Abigail's blackmail, something told me Margaret Wilkins was telling the truth.

"Do you know who else was on that list?" I asked.

She hesitated, glancing around the relatively empty square before responding. "I can't say for certain. Abigail wasn't foolish enough to share her leverage openly. But there were rumors. . ." She lowered her voice. "Mayor Wilson, for one. Something about improper allocation of town funds, though I don't know the details. And I suspect Chief Parker might have been on it too."

"The chief of police?" I was surprised. Chief Parker had always seemed like the epitome of small-town integrity.

Margaret nodded. "His son got into some trouble a few years back. The kind that might have resulted in jail time if it had been handled differently. Abigail's late husband was a judge, you know. Connections like that can make problems disappear."

My mind was racing, connecting dots I hadn't previously considered. "So Abigail had a collection of favors she could call in when needed."

"More like a collection of thumbscrews she could tighten," Margaret corrected grimly. "But yes, essentially."

"And her development project—the restoration plan for downtown—was she using these ... influences ... to push it through?"

"Without a doubt. The mayor's support was particularly crucial. The town council votes next week, and rumor has it she needed just one more vote to ensure it passed."

I remembered what Bunny had overheard between Abigail and Beau: "Fifty-fifty, no matter what they offer." If they were partners in the development project, both stood to profit significantly once it was approved.

"What about the Birdsong family?" I asked. "Were they involved in the project?"

Margaret's eyes narrowed shrewdly. "Now you're asking the right questions. The Birdsongs own a significant portion of the commercial real estate in this town, including several properties that would be affected by Abigail's plan. And young Beau has been branching out from the family business lately, making his own investments."

"With Abigail as a partner," I added, the pieces starting to fit together.

"So it would seem," she agreed. "Though that partnership might not have been entirely voluntary on Beau's part."

"You think she had something on him too?"

Margaret smiled thinly. "I think Abigail had something on everyone who mattered in this town. The question is, which of her victims finally decided they'd had enough?"

It was a good question—one I intended to find an answer to. "Thank you for being so candid, Mrs. Wilkins."

"Margaret, please." She patted my hand with surprising warmth. "And I hope you find what you're looking for, Lee. That Birdsong girl may be a walking disaster, but she doesn't deserve to be framed for murder."

As I stood to leave, a final thought occurred to me. "The poison in the chocolate—Detective Morrison mentioned it was a rare compound found in certain exotic plants. As head of the gardening club, would you know anything about that?"

Margaret's expression grew serious. "I might. There are several plants with toxic properties in our botanical collection at the community greenhouse. Mostly for educational purposes, you understand." She frowned thoughtfully. "I'd need to know exactly what compound was used to tell you more."

"I'll see what I can find out," I promised. "And Margaret? Thank you again."

She waved me off with a gardening glove. "Just be careful, Lee. Whoever killed Abigail probably isn't done tying up loose ends."

With that cheerful warning ringing in my ears, I headed back toward Heavenly Confections, my mind buzzing with new information. The list of potential suspects was growing: anyone Abigail had blackmailed might have wanted her silenced. But something about the method—poisoned chocolate that implicated Bunny—seemed too specific, too personal.

I was so absorbed in my thoughts that I almost collided with Detective Morrison as I rounded the corner near our shop.

"Ms. Woodyard," he greeted me, his expression inscrutable. "Just the person I was looking for."

"Detective," I acknowledged, trying not to look guilty despite having just been investigating behind his back. "What can I do for you?"

"I'd like you to come with me to the station," he said, his tone making it clear this wasn't a request. "We've uncovered some new evidence in Abigail Thornton's murder case that I think you'll find . . . illuminating."

A chill ran through me at his words. "What kind of evidence?"

Morrison's gaze was steady and unreadable. "Financial records showing significant payments from Abigail Thornton to various community members over the past year." A small, humorless smile played at his lips. "Including a rather large deposit to Heavenly Confections just last month."

My heart sank. Whatever was going on with Abigail's blackmail scheme and development project, it seemed our chocolate shop might be more deeply entangled than I had realized. And judging by Morrison's expression, explaining that connection was going to be anything but sweet.

Chapter 4: Cracked Shells

The police station was quieter than it had been that morning, with only a few officers moving purposefully through the reception area. Detective Morrison led me to the same small interview room where he'd questioned Bunny, but this time, the atmosphere felt decidedly more tense.

"Please, sit," he instructed, gesturing to the uncomfortable plastic chair I was beginning to know too well.

I complied, fighting to keep my expression neutral despite the anxiety churning in my stomach. "You mentioned financial records?"

Morrison placed a manila folder on the table between us but didn't open it immediately. Instead, he studied me with that unnerving, penetrating gaze of his.

"Ms. Woodyard, in my experience, small towns like Sweetwater Springs operate on two currencies: gossip and favors." He tapped the folder with one finger. "Abigail Thornton seems to have dealt extensively in both."

"So I've heard," I replied carefully.

His eyebrow arched slightly. "Have you? And what exactly have you heard?"

I hesitated, unsure how much to reveal about my conversation with Margaret. Detective Morrison was, after all, trying to solve a murder—the same thing I was attempting to do, albeit through less official channels. But he also seemed determined to build a case against Bunny, and possibly implicate Heavenly Confections in the process.

"Just rumors," I said finally. "That Abigail had leverage over various people in town. That she wasn't above using it to get what she wanted."

"Blackmail," Morrison clarified bluntly. "Let's call it what it was."

I nodded, relieved that he wasn't dancing around the issue. "Yes. Blackmail."

He opened the folder and turned it so I could see its contents—a series of bank statements and what appeared to be a handwritten ledger. "We found this in a hidden safe in Abigail's home office. It details payments to and from various individuals and businesses in Sweetwater Springs."

My eyes were immediately drawn to a highlighted entry: "Heavenly Confections—$5,000—Consultation Fee." The date was exactly one month ago.

"That's impossible," I said, the denial automatic and genuine. "We never received money from Abigail. Especially not that amount."

"The bank records confirm the transfer," Morrison countered, sliding another document toward me—a copy of a digital banking transaction showing exactly what he claimed: five thousand dollars transferred from Abigail Thornton's personal account to the business account of Heavenly Confections.

I stared at it, bewildered. "There must be some mistake. I would know if we'd received that kind of payment."

"Would you?" His tone was skeptical. "You share management duties with your aunt, correct? Is it possible she handled this transaction without informing you?"

The suggestion sent a jolt of indignation through me. "Absolutely not. Aunt Nettie and I don't keep financial secrets from each other. And we certainly wouldn't accept what amounts to a bribe from Abigail Thornton."

"A bribe for what, exactly?" Morrison leaned forward slightly. "What did Abigail want from Heavenly Confections that would be worth five thousand dollars?"

I shook my head, genuinely at a loss. "I have no idea. The only recent interaction we had with her was about her development project, and that was just the day before she died. She came to tell us our building might be sold and our rent increased."

"That hardly sounds like a relationship where she'd be paying you," Morrison observed dryly.

"Exactly! Which is why there must be a mistake with these records."

He studied me for a long moment, then gathered the papers back into the folder. "Well, perhaps your aunt can shed some light on the matter. I'll be speaking with her later today."

The thought of Aunt Nettie being questioned like a suspect made my heart race. "I want to be present for that conversation."

"That won't be possible," Morrison replied, his tone making it clear the matter wasn't up for discussion. "Now, there's something else I wanted to ask you about." He extracted a small evidence bag from his pocket and placed it on the table.

Inside was a small silver key. It looked ordinary except for a distinctive Easter egg charm attached to the key ring.

"Do you recognize this?" he asked.

I leaned closer, frowning. "It looks like the spare key to our storage closet at the shop. We keep extra supplies and seasonal decorations in there." I glanced up at him, confused. "Where did you find it?"

"In Abigail Thornton's purse," he answered, watching my reaction carefully. "Care to explain how it got there?"

My mind raced. "I have no idea. That key should be hanging on a hook in our office, along with other spare keys."

"When was the last time you saw it?"

I tried to remember, but honestly couldn't recall specifically checking for that particular key. "I don't know. We don't use the storage closet daily, especially not the spare key. Aunt Nettie and I both carry master keys for the shop."

Morrison made a note. "So Abigail Thornton had access to your storage closet, where you keep...?"

"Seasonal supplies, mostly," I explained. "Extra packaging materials, decorations, some older equipment we don't use regularly."

"And chocolate-making ingredients?" he pressed.

I saw where he was going with this and felt my defenses rise. "Basic ingredients, yes. Cocoa powder, some flavorings. But nothing that would explain a poisoned chocolate bunny, if that's what you're implying."

"I'm not implying anything, Ms. Woodyard. I'm following evidence." He returned the evidence bag to his pocket. "One more question: does Bunny Birdsong have access to this storage closet?"

"Technically, yes," I admitted reluctantly. "All employees have access to it, though Bunny rarely has reason to go in there. She mainly works the front counter and helps with basic kitchen prep."

Morrison nodded, making another note. "Thank you for your cooperation. You're free to go for now, but please don't leave town. We'll have more questions as the investigation progresses."

As I stood to leave, a thought occurred to me. "Detective, what was the poison used in the chocolate bunny? I know it triggered Abigail's peanut allergy, but you mentioned it was a rare compound found in certain plants."

He hesitated, apparently debating how much to share with me. "The lab results came back this morning. It was a concentrated extract of aconitum napellus—commonly known as monkshood or wolfsbane. Highly toxic in its own right, but especially dangerous to someone with Abigail's severe allergies."

"Monkshood," I repeated, recognizing the name. "Isn't that grown in the community greenhouse? For educational purposes?"

Morrison's gaze sharpened. "Your botanical knowledge is impressive, Ms. Woodyard. Yes, it is one of the specimens in the toxic plants section. Restricted access, supposedly."

"Margaret Wilkins would have access," I pointed out, then immediately regretted it. I hadn't meant to throw Margaret under the bus, especially after our candid conversation.

"Indeed she would," Morrison agreed. "Along with several other members of the gardening club. We're looking into all possibilities."

The way he emphasized "all" made it clear Bunny remained firmly at the top of his suspect list, despite the expanding circle of potential killers.

"Please give my aunt a call when you're ready to speak with her," I said as I headed for the door. "She'll be happy to explain the discrepancy in those financial records."

Morrison's only response was a noncommittal nod, which did nothing to ease my growing concern.

***

Outside the police station, I took a moment to gather my thoughts. The financial transfer and the key in Abigail's purse were troubling developments that suggested a connection between her and Heavenly Confections I hadn't been aware of. But what kind of connection? And did Aunt Nettie know about it?

I pulled out my phone to call her, then hesitated. This wasn't a conversation I wanted to have over the phone. Better to return to the shop and speak with her directly.

As I crossed the town square, I noticed a group gathered in front of the community center. A makeshift podium had been set up, and Mayor Wilson was addressing the crowd, his round face flushed with the importance of his role.

"—assure you that the Easter festival will proceed as planned," he was saying as I approached. "Abigail would have wanted it that way. In her honor, we will be establishing a memorial fund for downtown beautification, a cause that was dear to her heart."

I joined the back of the crowd, curious to hear what else the mayor might reveal. Standing near the front, I spotted Patricia Wilson, the mayor's wife, nodding approvingly at her husband's words. Tall and elegantly dressed, with an immaculate silver bob that matched her perfectly tailored suit, Patricia had always struck me as the power behind the throne in the Wilson marriage.

"Furthermore," the mayor continued, "the town council has decided to move forward with the vote on the Sweetwater Springs Restoration Project next week as scheduled. Abigail's vision for our community deserves our full consideration."

A murmur ran through the crowd—not entirely supportive, I noticed. Several business owners exchanged concerned glances. The restoration project, with its potential for increased rents and forced renovations, wasn't universally popular.

"Are there any questions?" Mayor Wilson asked, clearly hoping there wouldn't be.

Margaret Wilkins, who I hadn't noticed earlier, raised her hand. "Frank, is it appropriate to rush forward with this vote when the project's main architect has just died under suspicious circumstances? Shouldn't we take time to review the details more thoroughly?"

The mayor's smile tightened. "The project documentation is complete and has been available for review for weeks, Margaret. Delaying the vote would only cause unnecessary economic uncertainty for our community."

"Uncertainty for whom?" Margaret pressed. "The small businesses that might be priced out of their locations, or the investors waiting to profit from the development?"

Patricia Wilson stepped forward, placing a restraining hand on her husband's arm as he began to sputter an indignant response. "What Frank means," she interjected smoothly, "is that the project represents a significant opportunity for Sweetwater Springs. Abigail put her heart and soul into developing this plan. Moving forward with it honors her memory and her vision for our town."

Her calm, authoritative tone seemed to settle the crowd somewhat, though Margaret looked far from convinced. As the impromptu meeting broke up, I made my way toward the mayor and his wife, determined to learn more about their connection to Abigail's blackmail scheme.

"Mayor Wilson," I called, catching up to them as they descended from the podium. "Could I have a word?"

Frank Wilson looked distinctly uncomfortable at my approach, but Patricia's smile remained perfectly in place. "Lee Woodyard," she greeted me. "How is your aunt? I haven't seen Nettie at the library board meetings lately."

"She's been busy with Easter preparations," I explained. "Actually, I wanted to ask you both about Abigail Thornton's restoration project. It seems to be moving forward rather quickly."

"As it should," Patricia replied before her husband could speak. "It's a comprehensive plan for revitalizing our downtown area. The timing is unfortunate, of course, but progress can't stand still, even in the face of tragedy."

"I understand Abigail was particularly invested in getting the council's approval," I said carefully. "I hear she was quite . . . persuasive . . . with certain council members."

Mayor Wilson's face flushed an alarming shade of red. "What exactly are you implying, Ms. Woodyard?"

"I'm not implying anything," I assured him, though of course I was. "I'm just trying to understand the dynamics of the situation. Heavenly Confections has a stake in this too, since our building is part of the proposed renovation area."

Patricia's piercing blue eyes studied me with new interest. "Your concern for your business is understandable. Perhaps we could discuss this more privately? Frank has another appointment, but I'd be happy to walk you through the details of how the project will affect your specific location."

Her offer surprised me, but I wasn't about to pass up an opportunity for a private conversation with the mayor's wife—especially if Margaret's information about the mayor being on Abigail's blackmail list was accurate.

"That would be very helpful," I agreed.

Mayor Wilson looked relieved to be excused and hurried off after giving his wife a quick peck on the cheek. Patricia watched him go with an expression that might have been fondness or resignation, then turned back to me.

"Shall we walk? The spring air is delightful today."

We fell into step together, heading toward the less crowded edge of the town square where ornamental cherry trees were just beginning to bloom.

"I suppose you've heard the rumors," Patricia said without preamble once we were out of earshot of others.

I decided directness was my best approach. "About Abigail blackmailing your husband? Yes, I've heard them."

If I expected shock or denial, I was disappointed. Patricia merely nodded, her expression thoughtful. "Abigail was ... efficient ... in her methods. She understood that sometimes people need a little extra motivation to see the bigger picture."

"By 'extra motivation,' you mean threats and blackmail?" I couldn't keep the edge from my voice.

"That's a rather harsh characterization," she replied mildly. "Let's call it leveraging available resources. In Frank's case, there was a minor indiscretion involving town funds several years ago. Nothing criminal, merely ... improper. Abigail helped smooth things over, and in return, Frank offered his full support to her community initiatives."

The casual way she described what amounted to corruption was almost more shocking than the admission itself. "And you were okay with this arrangement?"

Patricia's smile was enigmatic. "Marriage is about partnership, Ms. Woodyard. Frank handles the public aspects of leadership; I handle the practical considerations behind the scenes. Abigail and I understood each other in that regard."

A chill ran through me as I realized the implication. "You were working with her on the restoration project."

"I prefer to think of it as a collaboration," she corrected. "Abigail had the vision and the financial backing. I have the connections and community insight. Together, we were creating something transformative for Sweetwater Springs."

"Transformative for whom?" I challenged, echoing Margaret's earlier question. "Small businesses like ours could be forced out by increased rents."

Patricia waved a dismissive hand. "Change always involves some displacement. But the economic benefits for the town as a whole will be substantial. Higher property values, increased tourism, more upscale retail options. . ."

"In other words, out with the old, in with the new," I summarized, not bothering to hide my displeasure.

"Progress isn't always comfortable," she acknowledged with a slight shrug. "But it is inevitable."

We had reached a small gazebo at the corner of the square, and Patricia gestured for me to join her on the bench inside. Once seated, her demeanor shifted subtly, becoming more focused, almost predatory.

"Now, let's discuss your situation," she said. "Heavenly Confections has been a charming fixture in our community for years, but let's be honest—artisanal chocolate shops are a dime a dozen these days. What makes yours special enough to survive in a more competitive marketplace?"

Her question caught me off guard. I'd expected more discussion about Abigail and the blackmail scheme, not a business consultation. "We have loyal customers, unique recipes passed down through generations, and a connection to this community that can't be replicated by some corporate chain."

"Sentiment doesn't pay rising rent," Patricia pointed out. "However, there might be a place for Heavenly Confections in the new vision for downtown—if you're willing to make certain . . . adjustments."

"What kind of adjustments?" I asked warily.

"A more upscale image. Specialized offerings. Perhaps a focus on 'bean-to-bar' or organic chocolates that would appeal to wealthy weekend tourists." She smiled, though it didn't reach her eyes. "Abigail had discussed creating a special fund to help selected businesses transition to the new model. I believe your aunt was aware of this opportunity."

The five-thousand-dollar "consultation fee" suddenly made more sense, though I still couldn't believe Aunt Nettie would accept such an arrangement without discussing it with me.

"Speaking of my aunt," I said carefully, "I should probably be getting back to the shop. We're short-staffed today."

Patricia nodded, accepting my obvious desire to end the conversation. "Of course. But do think about what I've said, Lee. The vote is next week, and after that, changes will happen quickly. Better to be on the right side of progress than swept away by it."

Her warning—for that's what it was, beneath the polite phrasing—hung in the air between us as I stood to leave.

"One more thing," I said, unable to resist pushing a little further. "The night Abigail died, where were you and the mayor?"

If I expected her to be flustered by the direct question, I was disappointed again. Patricia's smile remained perfectly in place. "At the hospital in Clayton. Frank had his quarterly cardiology check-up at 6:30. We didn't return to Sweetwater Springs until after 9 PM. The hospital staff can confirm our presence, as can Frank's doctor."

A solid alibi, then. I nodded my acknowledgment. "Thank you for your time, Mrs. Wilson."

"Patricia, please," she corrected smoothly. "And Lee? A bit of friendly advice: be careful about asking too many questions about

Abigail's death. Some answers might be more dangerous than you anticipate."

With that cryptic warning, she rose gracefully and headed back toward the community center, leaving me with more questions than answers.

***

When I finally returned to Heavenly Confections, I found the shop bustling with customers once again. Bunny was manning the register with surprising composure, while Aunt Nettie expertly wrapped Easter-themed gift boxes.

I caught my aunt's eye as I entered, and she gave me a slight nod that I interpreted as "wait until we're alone." I busied myself helping customers for the next hour until the afternoon rush subsided, and Aunt Nettie finally flipped the sign to "Closed" for our mid-afternoon preparation break.

"Bunny, can you start restocking the display cases?" she asked. "Lee and I need to check inventory in the office."

Once we were alone in the small room that served as our business office, Aunt Nettie closed the door and turned to me with an expression I'd rarely seen on her face: genuine worry.

"Detective Morrison called," she said without preamble. "He's coming by at five to question me about financial records. What's going on, Lee?"

I filled her in on everything: the five-thousand-dollar transfer, the key found in Abigail's purse, and my conversation with Patricia Wilson.

Aunt Nettie listened without interrupting, her normally cheerful face growing increasingly troubled. When I finished, she sank into her desk chair with a deep sigh.

"I was afraid of this," she murmured, almost to herself.

"Afraid of what?" I asked, a knot forming in my stomach. "Aunt Nettie, please tell me you didn't accept money from Abigail."

She looked up at me, her expression hurt. "Of course I didn't! But I was approached. About a month ago, Abigail invited me to lunch at the country club. She outlined her vision for the 'new' downtown Sweetwater Springs and suggested that Heavenly Confections might need to 'evolve' to fit into it."

"Patricia Wilson used almost the same words," I noted.

"I'm not surprised. Those two were thick as thieves when it came to this project." Aunt Nettie shook her head. "Anyway, Abigail offered what she called a 'transitional assistance grant' to help us 'upgrade' our image. Five thousand dollars as an initial consultation fee, with potentially more to follow if we cooperated with her vision."

"And you turned her down?" I prompted when she paused.

"I told her Heavenly Confections wasn't for sale—figuratively or literally. That we'd find a new location if necessary, but we wouldn't change our identity to fit her upscale tourist trap fantasy." A small, satisfied smile crossed her face at the memory. "She wasn't used to being refused. Called me shortsighted and provincial."

"But the bank records show the money was transferred to our business account," I pointed out.

Aunt Nettie frowned. "That's impossible. I never accepted the money, and I certainly never gave her our account information."

A cold realization dawned on me. "What if she transferred it anyway? To make it look like you'd accepted her offer? It would give her leverage."

"Blackmail," Aunt Nettie said grimly. "Just like with the others. If she could make it appear we'd taken a bribe, she could pressure us into supporting her plans for the building." She shook her head. "But our bank would have notified us of such a large deposit."

"Unless the notification went to the wrong email address," I suggested. "You know how the bank is always mixing up our contact information. Remember when they sent my new card to the shop's physical address instead of my home?"

"It's possible," she conceded. "But that still doesn't explain the key in her purse. I keep careful track of all our spare keys."

I moved to the pegboard where we hung various shop keys, each labeled with a small tag. The hook for the storage closet spare was empty.

"When did you last see it?" I asked.

Aunt Nettie joined me at the pegboard, frowning. "I honestly don't remember. We so rarely use that spare, and the storage closet isn't exactly high-security. It mainly contains extra packaging and seasonal decorations."

"And the recipe books," I reminded her. "Including your special formulations for nut-free chocolates."

Her eyes widened as she grasped the implication. "You think someone took the key to access our recipes? To learn how to make the Easter festival bunnies?"

"It would explain how the killer knew exactly how to craft a chocolate that mimicked our specialty bunnies," I reasoned. "And if they added the peanut oil and monkshood extract elsewhere, no one at the shop would be implicated in the actual poisoning."

"But who would go to such lengths?" Aunt Nettie wondered. "And why frame Bunny specifically?"

Before I could respond, there was a timid knock at the office door. Bunny poked her head in, her expression anxious.

"I'm sorry to interrupt, but there's someone here asking for you, Lee. He says it's urgent."

"Who is it?" I asked, already mentally running through a list of potential suspects or witnesses I needed to speak with.

"Mr. Jenkins," Bunny replied. "The landlord who owns our building? He seems really upset."

Aunt Nettie and I exchanged surprised glances. We'd been trying to reach Mr. Jenkins since yesterday to discuss Abigail's claim that he was selling the building.

"Send him in," Aunt Nettie decided. "This might be our chance to find out exactly what arrangement he had with Abigail."

A moment later, Elmer Jenkins shuffled into our office, looking every one of his seventy-eight years and then some. Normally a spry, cheerful man despite his age, today he seemed deflated, his usual dapper attire replaced by rumpled khakis and a cardigan that had seen better days.

"Nettie, Lee," he greeted us, his voice weary. "I came as soon as I heard about Abigail. Terrible business."

"Please, sit down," I offered, guiding him to the small armchair we kept for meetings with suppliers. "Can we get you anything? Coffee? Water?"

He waved away the offer. "No, no. I can't stay long. I just. . ." He trailed off, seemingly struggling to find the right words. "I needed to tell you in person. About the building."

My heart sank. "So it's true? You're selling to Abigail's development company?"

"Was," he corrected, looking miserable. "Was selling. The papers aren't finalized yet, but I did sign a preliminary agreement last week." He fidgeted with the edge of his cardigan. "I didn't want to, understand. This building has been in my family for generations. But Abigail . . . she was very persuasive."

"She blackmailed you," Aunt Nettie stated simply, no judgment in her tone.

Mr. Jenkins's head snapped up, his weathered face flushing. "How did you know?"

"It seems to have been her standard operating procedure," I explained gently. "What did she have on you, Mr. Jenkins?"

He sighed deeply, shoulders slumping. "Tax issues from the 1990s. Nothing criminal, mind you, but . . . creative accounting that wouldn't stand up to serious scrutiny. She somehow got hold of my old records and threatened to turn them over to the IRS if I didn't sell to her at below market value."

"I'm so sorry," Aunt Nettie said, genuine sympathy in her voice. "That must have been incredibly stressful."

"It was," he admitted. "But that's not why I'm here. I wanted to let you know that without Abigail pushing the sale through, I'm backing out. The building stays as is, and your lease remains unchanged." He managed a small smile. "No rent increases, no fancy renovations, no 'artisanal chocolate boutique' nonsense."

Relief flooded through me. At least one crisis had been averted. "Thank you, Mr. Jenkins. That means more than you know."

"It's the least I can do," he replied, some of his usual spirit returning. "You Woodyard women have been model tenants for decades. I'm not about to toss you out because some city-minded developer thinks Sweetwater Springs needs to be 'modernized.'"

As heartening as his loyalty was, I couldn't help wondering about the timing of his visit. "Mr. Jenkins, not that we're not grateful for the news, but why the urgency to tell us today?"

His expression clouded. "The police came to see me this morning. Asked all sorts of questions about Abigail, the building sale, who knew about it." He lowered his voice, though we were alone in the office. "They seemed particularly interested in whether I'd told anyone about Abigail's blackmail scheme."

"Had you?" I asked.

He shook his head emphatically. "Not a soul. Too embarrassed, if I'm being honest. But. . ." he hesitated, "I did confront her about it, the day before she died. Told her I was considering fighting the sale, blackmail be damned."

"How did she respond?" Aunt Nettie asked.

"Laughed in my face," Mr. Jenkins recalled bitterly. "Said she had bigger leverage than just my tax problems. Something about a list of community members who'd be very unhappy if I disrupted her plans." He frowned at the memory. "She implied she had half the town in her pocket, one way or another."

The infamous list again. I was becoming increasingly convinced that this list—and the secrets it contained—was central to Abigail's murder.

"Did she mention any names specifically?" I pressed.

"Just one," Mr. Jenkins replied. "Said even if I went to the authorities, it wouldn't matter because Chief Parker 'understood the value of discretion.' Made it sound like he was in her pocket too."

This aligned with what Margaret had told me about the police chief's son having some legal trouble that had been smoothed over. The web of Abigail's influence seemed to extend into every corner of Sweetwater Springs.

"Mr. Jenkins," I said carefully, "where were you yesterday evening, around 6:30 to 7:30?"

He didn't seem offended by the question. "Fishing at Miller's Pond, same as I am most evenings when the weather's good. Caught three decent-sized bass." He offered a small smile.

"Already told the police all this. My neighbor Harold can confirm it—he was there with me."

Another solid alibi. I was beginning to think everyone in town except Bunny had an ironclad account of their whereabouts at the time of Abigail's death.

"Thank you for coming by," Aunt Nettie said warmly as Mr. Jenkins rose to leave. "And thank you for standing by us. It means a great deal."

He patted her hand affectionately. "You Woodyard women are part of what makes this town special. Don't you forget it."

After he left, Aunt Nettie and I remained in thoughtful silence for a moment.

"Well," she said finally, "that's one problem solved, at least. Our shop is safe for now."

"But the mystery of Abigail's murder is getting more complicated, not less," I pointed out. "She had half the town blackmailed or bribed, a mysterious business partnership with Beau Birdsong, and was killed with poison from the community greenhouse in a chocolate made from our recipe."

"And Detective Morrison thinks we were involved," Aunt Nettie added grimly. "Either because of a bribe we supposedly accepted or because of our connection to Bunny."

"We need to find that list," I decided. "The complete version. It could tell us who had the strongest motive to want Abigail silenced permanently."

Aunt Nettie nodded, her expression resolute. "Agreed. But how? The police would have the original, assuming it was among Abigail's effects."

I thought for a moment, then remembered something Patricia Wilson had said. "Patricia mentioned that Abigail had a home office. That must be where the police found the financial records.

Maybe there are other clues there that they missed or haven't connected yet."

"Lee Woodyard," my aunt said with a mix of admiration and concern, "are you suggesting we break into a dead woman's house?"

"Of course not," I assured her, though the thought had briefly crossed my mind. "But I am suggesting we find a legitimate reason to visit. Didn't you mention once that you and Abigail served together on the library fundraising committee?"

Understanding dawned in Aunt Nettie's eyes. "Yes, three years ago. We organized the annual book sale together. I still have some of her files that I never returned—templates for donor letters and such."

"Well, what better time to finally return them than now?" I suggested innocently. "It would be the neighborly thing to do, helping Abigail's family sort through her affairs."

"Except Abigail has no family in Sweetwater Springs," Aunt Nettie pointed out. "Her nearest relative is a niece in Seattle."

"Then we'll offer to help Patricia Wilson," I countered. "She and Abigail were 'thick as thieves,' as you put it. She's probably handling the personal effects."

Aunt Nettie looked skeptical. "And you think Patricia will just let us wander around Abigail's house, potentially discovering her blackmail materials?"

"No," I admitted. "But it gets us in the door. And once we're inside. . ." I left the implication hanging.

"You've been reading too many mystery novels," my aunt sighed, though I could tell she wasn't entirely opposed to the idea. "But we have a more immediate problem to solve. Detective Morrison will be here at five, expecting an explanation for that five-thousand-dollar transfer I never authorized or received."

"I think I have a solution for that too," I said, an idea forming. "But we'll need Bunny's help."

"Why Bunny?"

"Because," I explained, "if I'm right about who's behind all this, Bunny might be the key to proving it—and clearing all our names in the process."

Just then, the front bell jingled, signaling a customer despite our "Closed" sign. Bunny's voice floated back to us, apologetic but firm. "I'm so sorry, but we're closed for our afternoon preparation break. We'll reopen at—oh! Detective Morrison. You're early."

Aunt Nettie and I exchanged alarmed glances. The detective wasn't due for another two hours.

"Showtime," I murmured, squeezing her hand reassuringly before we headed out to face what promised to be a very uncomfortable interrogation.

But as we stepped into the main shop area, I was surprised to see Detective Morrison wasn't alone. Standing beside him, looking uncomfortable but determined, was Beau Birdsong.

"Ms. Woodyard," Morrison greeted me, his expression unreadable as always. "Mr. Birdsong has something he'd like to share with us. Something about Abigail Thornton's murder that changes everything."

Beau's eyes met mine, and for the first time since I'd known him, the polished veneer had cracked, revealing something that looked suspiciously like fear underneath.

"I know who killed Abigail," he said quietly. "And why they tried to frame Bunny for it."

The tension in the room was palpable as we all waited for him to continue. Whatever revelation was coming, I had a feeling it would turn our investigation—and perhaps the entire town of Sweetwater Springs—upside down.

Chapter 5: Dark Chocolate Secrets

The silence that followed Beau's declaration seemed to stretch for an eternity. Through the plate glass window of Heavenly Confections, I could see the late afternoon sun casting long shadows across the town square, the cheerful Easter decorations suddenly appearing garish rather than festive.

"Perhaps we should continue this conversation somewhere more private," Detective Morrison suggested, his eyes scanning the shop where Bunny stood frozen behind the counter, her face drained of color.

"My office," Aunt Nettie offered, her voice remarkably steady despite the tension. She turned to Bunny with a reassuring smile. "Could you finish restocking the display cases? We'll reopen at 5:30 as planned."

Bunny nodded mutely, her wide eyes fixed on her estranged husband. The look that passed between them was impossible to decipher—not quite hatred, not quite fear, but a complex mixture of emotions that spoke volumes about their shared history.

In the cramped confines of our office, Detective Morrison positioned himself by the door while Beau took the visitor's chair. Aunt Nettie and I stood side by side, unconsciously presenting a united front.

"Alright, Mr. Birdsong," Morrison prompted. "Tell them what you told me."

Beau ran a hand through his immaculately styled hair, a gesture that somehow made him appear more human than I'd ever seen him. The polished facade had cracked, revealing uncertainty beneath.

"I've been ... working with Abigail on her downtown restoration project," he began, his usual smooth tone roughened by what sounded like genuine distress. "Not by choice, initially. She approached me about six months ago with evidence of certain ... irregularities in some of my real estate dealings."

"She blackmailed you," I translated bluntly.

He winced but nodded. "Yes. I'd leveraged some properties in ways that wouldn't stand up to regulatory scrutiny. Nothing illegal, exactly, but definitely in the gray area. Abigail threatened to expose everything unless I became her partner in the restoration project."

"Partner in what sense?" Aunt Nettie asked.

"Officially, my role was to help secure property agreements and navigate zoning regulations using my family's connections," Beau explained. "Unofficially, I was the front man for her less savory tactics. When someone refused to cooperate, I'd find leverage—financial problems, personal indiscretions, family secrets." His expression turned bitter. "Abigail called it 'community research.'"

"You helped her blackmail half the town," I summarized, disgust evident in my voice.

Beau didn't deny it. "It started small—a few nudges to get the initial approvals. But Abigail became increasingly aggressive. The more power she accumulated, the more she wanted." He looked directly at Aunt Nettie. "Your building was particularly important to her plans. The corner location, the historical facade—it was meant to be the showcase for the whole project."

"Mr. Jenkins already told us about the blackmail," I said. "What does any of this have to do with Abigail's murder?"

Beau shifted uncomfortably. "Three days ago, I discovered something disturbing in Abigail's home office. I was dropping off some documents when she stepped out to take a call. Her computer was open to a spreadsheet—not the official project financials, but a separate accounting. It showed projections for property acquisitions after the restoration was complete."

"I don't understand," Aunt Nettie said, frowning.

"The restoration project was just phase one," Beau clarified. "Once the downtown area was 'revitalized' and property values increased, Abigail planned to systematically buy out most of the original business owners at deflated prices. She'd created financial profiles for each target, calculating exactly how much pressure it would take to force them to sell."

The implications were chilling. "She was orchestrating an entire economic takeover of Sweetwater Springs," I realized aloud.

« With certain partners who stood to profit enormously, » Beau confirmed. « But there was a twist I didn't know about until I saw that spreadsheet. My name wasn't among those partners. »

"She was going to cut you out," Detective Morrison interjected, speaking for the first time since we'd entered the office.

Beau nodded grimly. "Once my usefulness ended, I'd be discarded—or worse, implicated if any of the blackmail schemes came to light. Abigail kept meticulous records of everyone's involvement, including mine. Insurance, she called it."

"The list everyone's been whispering about," I said.

"More than a list," Beau corrected. "A detailed dossier on every person of consequence in Sweetwater Springs, complete with documentation of their secrets and weaknesses. And a second list of her accomplices in the scheme."

"Which included you," Aunt Nettie observed.

"And Patricia Wilson," Beau added, confirming my suspicions from earlier. "She was Abigail's true partner in all this. The political muscle behind the financial manipulation."

Detective Morrison cleared his throat. "Mr. Birdsong, please get to the information directly relevant to the murder."

Beau straightened in his chair. "When I confronted Abigail about her plans to cut me out, she laughed it off. Said I was never more than a useful tool with a good family name. When I threatened to expose her, she pointed out that I was implicated in everything she'd done. My reputation would be destroyed along with hers."

"So you killed her," I suggested, watching his reaction carefully.

"No!" Beau's denial was vehement. "I was angry, yes, but murder wasn't the solution. I needed leverage of my own—something to neutralize the threat she posed."

"The list," Aunt Nettie guessed.

He nodded. "I decided to find her master file—the complete record of all her schemes. I thought if I had a copy, we'd be at a stalemate. She couldn't destroy me without risking herself."

"But someone else got to her first," Detective Morrison supplied.

"Yes," Beau confirmed, his gaze shifting to me. "The same person who's been trying to frame Bunny for the murder."

My pulse quickened. "Who?"

"Patricia Wilson." Beau's answer hung in the air like a thunderclap. "She and Abigail had a falling out over the final distribution of properties. Patricia wanted certain businesses preserved—ones owned by her personal friends or political allies. Abigail refused to make exceptions."

The conversation I'd had with Patricia earlier took on new significance. Her calm assurance about the project moving forward despite Abigail's death, her pointed warnings about asking too many questions—it all pointed to someone protecting their interests.

"Do you have evidence of this?" Morrison asked, his professional skepticism evident.

Beau reached into his jacket pocket and withdrew a small flash drive. "This is what I came to warn Bunny about yesterday. I managed to download a portion of Abigail's records before I left her house that day. There's a file detailing Patricia's involvement and the growing conflict between them."

"Why would Patricia frame Bunny specifically?" I asked, still not entirely convinced. "What's the connection?"

"Two reasons," Beau replied. "First, Patricia knew about my relationship with Abigail through the restoration project. If suspicion fell on Bunny as a jealous soon-to-be-ex-wife, it would indirectly implicate me as well, removing both of us as potential threats."

"And the second reason?" Aunt Nettie prompted.

Beau's expression turned pained. "Bunny knows things. Things she overheard during our marriage that could connect Patricia to some of the more questionable aspects of town governance over the years. Bunny never understood the significance of what she heard, but if she ever pieced it together..." He trailed off meaningfully.

I remembered Bunny mentioning the "conditions" attached to her divorce settlement offers—keeping quiet about "certain things." It was starting to make a terrible kind of sense.

"That's why you've been pressuring her in the divorce," I realized. "Not out of spite, but to ensure her silence."

"It was for her protection as much as mine," Beau insisted, though the justification rang hollow. "Patricia Wilson doesn't hesitate to eliminate problems. I didn't want Bunny to become one."

Detective Morrison took the flash drive from Beau with a latex-gloved hand. "This will need to be verified by our technical team. In the meantime, Mr. Birdsong, you'll need to provide a formal statement at the station."

"Of course," Beau agreed readily. "But there's one more thing you should know. The five-thousand-dollar transfer to Heavenly Confections? It wasn't authorized by Nettie Woodyard. Abigail made the transfer anyway and falsified documentation to make it appear as if Nettie had accepted a bribe. It was part of her standard operating procedure—creating evidence of complicity before it actually existed."

Aunt Nettie exhaled sharply. "I knew I never accepted that money!"

"The funds are still in your account," Morrison pointed out. "If you didn't authorize the transfer, why didn't you report it or return it?"

"Because we didn't know about it," I explained. "The bank must have sent notification to an incorrect email address. It happens all the time with our business account."

Morrison made a note. "We'll verify that with the bank. Now, about the key found in Abigail's possession—"

"That was me," Beau admitted, surprising us all. "I took it from your shop during a visit last month and gave it to Abigail. She wanted access to your storage area to . . . well, to plant evidence if necessary. Make it look like you were involved in something unethical if you refused to cooperate with her plans."

The casual way he confessed to what amounted to conspiracy left me speechless with anger. This man had been willing to destroy our reputation, our livelihood, all to protect his own interests.

"You do realize you're confessing to criminal activity," Morrison said mildly.

Beau nodded. "I'm aware. But at this point, coming clean is my only chance to protect myself—and Bunny." He glanced at me, something like genuine regret in his eyes. "For what it's worth, I'm sorry for my part in this. Abigail had a way of making you feel like you had no choice but to play by her rules."

I wasn't inclined toward forgiveness, but there were more pressing matters at hand. "If Patricia killed Abigail, how did she get one of our chocolate bunnies? And how did she know to poison it with monkshood and peanut oil?"

"The chocolate was easy," Beau explained. "Patricia is on the Easter festival committee. She had access to the special bunnies Nettie made for their meeting. As for the poison. . ." He hesitated.

"Go on," Morrison prompted.

"Patricia's sister was a botanical researcher before she retired. She literally wrote a book on toxic plants. And Patricia is an honorary member of the gardening club—she would have access to the greenhouse where the monkshood is grown."

The pieces were falling into place, but something still bothered me. "Why kill Abigail now? Why not wait until after the town council vote secured the restoration project?"

"Because Abigail was planning to expose several council members at the meeting scheduled for the day after she died," Beau revealed. "She was tired of negotiating with Patricia over which properties to target. She planned to use her blackmail material to force a unanimous vote without any further compromises."

"So Patricia eliminated her before she could follow through," Aunt Nettie concluded. "And the restoration project still moves forward, but now under Patricia's control."

"With none of Abigail's planned exclusions for Patricia's allies," Beau added. "It was a power play disguised as a murder investigation."

Detective Morrison had been taking notes throughout this explanation. Now he closed his notebook decisively. "This is all very interesting, Mr. Birdsong, but remains largely speculative without corroborating evidence. The flash drive may help, but we'll need more."

"What about Bunny's scarf?" I asked. "How would Patricia have gotten that to plant at the crime scene?"

Beau looked uncomfortable. "That might have been me, indirectly. I mentioned to Patricia that Bunny always leaves her scarves hanging by the back door at the shop. I didn't think anything of it at the time—it was just conversation about Bunny's absentminded habits."

"Giving Patricia the perfect way to frame her," I said disgustedly.

Morrison checked his watch. "We should continue this discussion at the station. Mr. Birdsong, if you'll come with me—"

The office door burst open, startling us all. Bunny stood in the doorway, her eyes wide with panic.

"Someone left this on the front counter," she said breathlessly, holding up a small package wrapped in festive Easter paper. "It wasn't there before, I swear. Someone must have come in while we were all back here."

Morrison crossed the room in two quick strides, taking the package from her hands. "Did you see who delivered it?"

Bunny shook her head. "No, I was arranging truffles in the display case. When I turned around, it was just . . . there."

The detective examined the package carefully. It was about the size of a paperback book, wrapped in pastel paper decorated with cartoon Easter bunnies. A small gift tag attached to the top read simply: "For Lee."

"It's addressed to you," Morrison said, looking at me with concern. "Did you see anyone approach the shop in the last few minutes?"

"No," I replied, a chill running down my spine. "The shop was empty when we came back here."

Morrison placed the package on the desk and carefully pulled back one corner of the wrapping paper with his pen. Inside was a familiar shape—one of our signature chocolate bunnies with the Easter festival logo emblazoned on its stomach.

"Nobody touch it," he ordered, though none of us had made a move to do so. "I'm calling this in. We need the forensics team here immediately."

As he stepped aside to make the call, Aunt Nettie moved closer to examine the chocolate without touching it. "That's definitely one of our festival bunnies," she confirmed. "But all of those were accounted for. We made exactly twelve for the committee meeting."

"Eleven were picked up by Abigail," I recalled. "The twelfth was the one found with her body."

"Then this is a replica," Beau suggested, keeping his distance from the suspicious package. "Made to look like your special design."

"A warning," I said softly, realization dawning. "Someone's letting me know that I could be next if I keep asking questions."

Morrison rejoined us, his expression grim. "Forensics will be here in twenty minutes. In the meantime, I'm evacuating the building as a precaution. This could be more than a warning—it could be an active threat."

Aunt Nettie's face paled. "You mean it might be. . ."

"Poisoned, yes," Morrison confirmed. "Possibly with the same substance that killed Abigail Thornton."

As we filed out of the office, Bunny hung back, her expression troubled. "Lee, there's something else. When I found the package, I also noticed this." She held up a small piece of paper that appeared to have been torn from a notebook. "It was on the floor near the counter."

I took it from her, careful to touch only the edges. The handwriting was elegant and precise, the ink a distinctive shade of blue. "Loose ends must be tied before Easter," it read. "No exceptions."

"That's Patricia's handwriting," Beau said, leaning over my shoulder to see the note. "I recognize it from council documents she's drafted."

I handed the note to Morrison, who placed it in an evidence bag. "If this is genuine, it could be the corroboration we need to obtain a search warrant for the Wilson residence."

"You think Patricia left it deliberately?" Aunt Nettie asked skeptically.

"No," I said, a theory forming in my mind. "I think she wrote this as a reminder to herself, not realizing she'd dropped it when she left the chocolate. It's not a confession—it's a to-do list."

"And we're the loose ends," Bunny whispered, her face ghost-white.

Morrison ushered us toward the exit. "All the more reason to get everyone to safety. Mr. Birdsong, you'll be coming to the station with me to make a formal statement. Ms. Woodyard—both Ms. Woodyards—and Ms. Birdsong will be escorted to a secure location until we determine the nature of this threat."

Outside, the late afternoon sunshine seemed at odds with the dark turn of events. As we waited for the forensics team and police escort to arrive, I pulled Aunt Nettie and Bunny aside.

"We need to be very careful," I warned them quietly. "If Patricia Wilson is behind this, she has connections throughout the town—including within the police department."

"Chief Parker," Aunt Nettie murmured, remembering our earlier discussion about Abigail's leverage over the police chief.

"Exactly. We can't be sure who we can trust." I glanced at Detective Morrison, who was speaking urgently into his radio a few yards away. "Except possibly Morrison. He's new to town and doesn't seem to have any local ties."

"What should we do?" Bunny asked, her voice steadier than I expected given the circumstances.

I thought quickly. "We play along with the police protection for now. But we keep our eyes open and our mouths shut about any theories or evidence until we know who's on which side."

"And the Easter festival?" Aunt Nettie asked. "It starts tomorrow with the children's egg decorating workshop. The main events are all weekend."

I'd almost forgotten about the festival with everything else happening. "We should assume it's going forward. Patricia won't want to disrupt the town's normal activities—that would draw unwanted attention. In fact. . ." I paused as a new thought struck me. "The festival might be exactly what we need."

"How so?" Bunny asked.

"It puts Patricia in the public eye," I explained. "She'll be playing the role of grieving colleague while secretly finalizing her takeover plans. If we can find evidence connecting her to Abigail's murder during the festival, she won't be able to quietly dispose of it—or us."

Aunt Nettie nodded slowly. "The USB drive Beau gave Morrison might be enough, if it contains what he claims."

"We can't count on that," I cautioned. "We need something definitive—something that proves beyond doubt that Patricia poisoned that chocolate bunny."

"But how do we find that kind of evidence in the middle of a town festival?" Bunny wondered.

Before I could answer, Morrison approached with two uniformed officers. "Your escort is here. They'll take you to a hotel in Clayton until we've assessed the threat."

"Clayton?" I protested. "That's thirty miles away. What about our shop? The Easter festival starts tomorrow, and we have orders to fill."

"Your safety takes priority over chocolate bunnies, Ms. Woodyard," Morrison replied firmly.

I was about to argue further when Aunt Nettie placed a restraining hand on my arm. "The detective is right, Lee. We can notify our customers about the delay once we're settled."

Her meaningful look told me she had something else in mind. I nodded reluctantly, playing along. "Fine. But we'll need to stop by the house to pack a few things."

"Officers Grant and Perez will escort you," Morrison agreed. "Stay within their sight at all times, understood? Once forensics has cleared your shop, we'll know more about what we're dealing with."

As we were led to the waiting police car, I glanced back at Heavenly Confections. Through the window, I could see the threatening chocolate bunny still sitting on our office desk, a sweet-looking harbinger of danger. Somehow, our cozy chocolate shop had become the epicenter of a power struggle that threatened the entire town.

"Don't worry," Aunt Nettie murmured as we settled into the backseat of the police cruiser. "Chocolate may melt under pressure, but Woodyards don't."

***

The drive to our Victorian house took only a few minutes. Officer Grant, a serious young woman with a no-nonsense demeanor, accompanied us inside while her partner remained with the car.

"Please be quick," she advised. "Pack only essentials for a day or two."

In my bedroom, I hastily threw some clothes into an overnight bag, my mind racing through possibilities. If we were taken to Clayton, we'd be effectively removed from the investigation at a critical juncture. Patricia would have free rein to tie up her "loose ends" before Easter—which was only three days away.

Aunt Nettie appeared in my doorway, her own bag in hand. "Officer Grant is waiting in the living room," she said at a normal volume, then lowered her voice to a near whisper. "I have a plan, but we'll need a distraction."

"What kind of distraction?" I whispered back.

"Something to separate our police escorts temporarily. Once we're at the hotel in Clayton—"

A soft knock interrupted us as Bunny joined our whispered conference. "Sorry, but I think we might have a bigger problem," she murmured. "I just got a text from Beau." She held up her phone, displaying a message that made my blood run cold.

"Patricia just called emergency town council meeting for tonight. Vote on restoration moved up. Don't trust the police escort."

"How would she know about our police escort so quickly?" I wondered.

"Unless she arranged it," Aunt Nettie concluded grimly. "Remember what Margaret said about Chief Parker owing Abigail favors? If Patricia inherited Abigail's leverage. . ."

The implications were chilling. We might be walking into a trap rather than protective custody.

"Ms. Woodyard? Ms. Birdsong?" Officer Grant called from downstairs. "We need to get moving."

Bunny's eyes were wide with fear. "What do we do?"

I made a split-second decision. "We need to split up. Aunt Nettie, you go with the officers. Maintain the appearance that everything is normal. Bunny and I will find another way out."

"Absolutely not," Aunt Nettie protested. "I'm not leaving you two alone to face whatever Patricia has planned."

"We don't have time to argue," I insisted. "If all three of us disappear, they'll know something's wrong immediately. This way, you can buy us some time."

"And put myself directly in Patricia's hands? No thank you."

"You'll be with legitimate police officers in a public hotel," I reasoned. "Patricia can't touch you there without exposing herself. Meanwhile, Bunny and I can gather evidence to clear her name and implicate Patricia."

Aunt Nettie's expression remained stubborn. "It's too dangerous."

"Ladies?" Officer Grant's voice was closer now, her footsteps audible on the stairs.

"Fine," Aunt Nettie relented with clear reluctance. "But you check in every hour, understood? And at the first sign of real danger, you call Detective Morrison directly."

I nodded quickly. "Deal. Now go stall the officer while we slip out the back."

As Aunt Nettie intercepted Officer Grant in the hallway with questions about what to pack for the hotel stay, Bunny and I crept toward the rear staircase that led to the kitchen. From there, a seldom-used door opened onto the side yard, partially concealed by a tall hedge.

"Where are we going?" Bunny whispered as we eased the door open, wincing at its slight creak.

"First, somewhere Patricia won't think to look for us," I replied. "Then, to find the evidence we need before the council vote tonight."

We slipped out into the gathering dusk, keeping low as we moved along the hedge line toward the neighboring property. My heart was pounding so loudly I was certain Officer Perez would hear it from his position in the front of the house, but we made it to the street behind ours without raising an alarm.

"Now what?" Bunny asked, her voice shaky but determined.

I pulled out my phone. "Now we call the one person in town who has nothing to lose by helping us. The one person who might have access to exactly what we need."

"Who?"

"Margaret Wilkins," I said decisively. "If anyone knows where to find proof of Patricia's crimes, it's the woman who's been watching her schemes unfold for decades."

As I dialed Margaret's number, I couldn't help but think of the chocolate bunny left as a warning on our counter. Whoever had planted it—presumably Patricia or someone working for her—had made a critical error. They'd underestimated just how far two chocolate-makers and a clumsy shop assistant would go to protect their own.

Patricia Wilson might be a master manipulator with half the town in her pocket, but she was about to discover that in Sweetwater Springs, even the sweetest treats could hide a bitter surprise.

Chapter 6: The Final Bite

Darkness had fallen by the time Margaret Wilkins ushered us through her back door into a kitchen that smelled pleasantly of herbal tea and freshly baked bread. Despite the late hour and our unexpected arrival, she remained remarkably composed, her gray hair neatly pulled back, her cardigan buttoned perfectly.

"I was wondering when you'd come to me," she said, gesturing for us to sit at her small kitchen table. "Though I didn't expect you to arrive as fugitives."

"We're not exactly fugitives," I protested weakly.

Margaret arched a skeptical eyebrow. "No? Then why are you sneaking through my garden at eight o'clock in the evening instead of being safely tucked away in police protection?"

News travels impossibly fast in small towns. "How did you know about the police protection?"

"Patricia called an emergency meeting of all committee heads an hour ago," Margaret explained, placing cups of tea before us that neither Bunny nor I had asked for. "She announced that due to a 'credible threat' against festival organizers, police would be providing security throughout the weekend. She specifically mentioned that you two and your aunt had already been moved to a secure location."

Bunny's eyes widened. "But we only just escaped from the police escort."

"Exactly," Margaret said grimly. "Which means Patricia had already arranged for you to be . . . dealt with . . . once you reached your destination."

A chill ran through me that had nothing to do with the cooling spring evening. "We think the police chief might be compromised. Abigail had leverage over him regarding his son, and Patricia seems to have inherited all of Abigail's blackmail material."

"Not all of it," Margaret corrected, disappearing briefly into an adjacent room. She returned with a leather-bound notebook, which she placed carefully on the table between us. "Abigail wasn't just methodical; she was paranoid. She kept physical backups of her most important information, distributed among people she thought she could control."

I stared at the notebook. "And she gave one to you?"

"Not willingly," Margaret's smile was sharp as a thorn. "Let's just say I've had practice retrieving things that don't belong to me. In my youth, I was quite adept at . . . liberating . . . items of interest."

Bunny gaped at her. "You stole Abigail's blackmail notebook?"

"I prefer to think of it as insurance," Margaret sniffed. "When you've lived as long as I have in a town this size, you learn to protect yourself. Especially from people like Abigail Thornton."

I reached for the notebook, but Margaret placed a restraining hand over mine. "Before you look at this, understand what you're getting into. This contains secrets that could destroy lives—not just Patricia's, but many respected members of this community. Once you know these things, you can't un-know them."

"We don't care about anyone else's secrets," I assured her. "We only need evidence linking Patricia to Abigail's murder."

Margaret studied me intently before slowly withdrawing her hand. "Very well. But remember—knowledge is a burden as well as a weapon."

The notebook was filled with Abigail's precise handwriting, organized by family name with dates, transactions, and leverage points meticulously documented. I flipped to the section marked "Wilson" and began to read, Bunny peering over my shoulder.

"Oh my God," Bunny whispered as we scanned the pages. "Patricia has been manipulating town affairs for decades. Way before Abigail ever came to Sweetwater Springs."

"Abigail didn't create the system," Margaret confirmed. "She merely perfected it. Patricia has been the power behind every mayor since she married Frank Wilson fifteen years ago. What Abigail brought to the table was outside investment money and a more . . . aggressive approach."

I continued reading, the picture becoming clearer with each page. Patricia had orchestrated zoning changes, property devaluations, and strategic foreclosures for years, gradually consolidating control over key areas of Sweetwater Springs. Abigail's restoration project was meant to be the culminating move—a complete economic restructuring of the town that would leave them controlling virtually every significant commercial property.

"Here," I said, pointing to an entry dated just one week before Abigail's murder. "It says Patricia and Abigail had a 'fundamental disagreement over final distribution of Phase Two properties.' " I looked up at Margaret. "What's Phase Two?"

"The real plan," she explained. "After the restoration project increased property values, they would force out most of the original businesses in favor of corporate chains and upscale boutiques. But apparently, Patricia wanted to protect certain properties—ones owned by her allies or family connections."

"And Abigail refused," I continued, seeing where this was heading. "She was going to expose several council members at a meeting scheduled for the day after she died, to force a unanimous vote without any compromises."

"That's how Beau explained it," Bunny confirmed, her normally cheerful face solemn. "Abigail was tired of negotiating with Patricia."

"So Patricia eliminated her before she could follow through," I finished. "But is there anything in here that directly links Patricia to the murder itself? Motive is one thing, but we need physical evidence."

Margaret gestured for me to continue turning pages. Near the back of the notebook, I found a section titled "Insurance Policies" with a list of storage locations and keys. One entry caught my eye immediately: "Greenhouse supply cabinet—extra monkshood specimens for botanical display."

"The poison," I breathed. "Abigail was keeping extra monkshood in the greenhouse, where Patricia would have access as an honorary gardening club member."

"Not just keeping it," Margaret clarified. "Documenting it as part of her insurance policy. Abigail knew exactly what Patricia was capable of. She was preparing for the possibility of betrayal."

"But she didn't move fast enough," Bunny said softly.

"There's more," I said, reading the final entry, dated the very day of Abigail's murder. "It says, 'P.W. accessed botanical cabinet 10:30 AM. Surveillance system captured clear images. Backup stored in Easter flash drive.'"

Margaret's eyes widened. "Abigail had surveillance in the greenhouse? That's . . . that would be definitive proof."

"If we can find this Easter flash drive," I agreed, excitement building. "But where would she hide something like that?"

Bunny had been unusually quiet, but now she spoke up. "The Easter festival. Abigail was in charge of it this year. What if the flash drive is hidden somewhere in the festival preparations?"

It made a certain twisted sense. Hiding crucial evidence in plain sight, surrounded by Easter-themed decorations and activities, would be both clever and secure. No one would think to look for incriminating evidence in a box of pastel eggs or festival supplies.

"The Easter egg hunt," I realized suddenly. "That's tomorrow morning in the town square. What if the flash drive is disguised as an Easter egg or hidden inside one of the eggs?"

"That would be too risky," Margaret countered. "Too easy for a child to find it accidentally."

"Not necessarily," I argued. "The eggs for tomorrow's hunt are being stored in the community center overnight. Patricia is chairing the committee meeting there right now. She'd have perfect access to remove the flash drive before the hunt begins."

"Or she already has," Bunny pointed out.

I shook my head. "I don't think so. If she'd found Abigail's backup evidence, she wouldn't still be trying to eliminate us. She'd be confident that no proof remained."

Margaret checked her watch. "The emergency council meeting is scheduled to start in thirty minutes. Patricia will be moving the vote on the restoration project forward before anyone can organize opposition."

"Then we need to get to the community center now," I decided, standing up. "If the flash drive is hidden among the Easter preparations, that's our best chance to find it before Patricia does."

"And if it's not there?" Bunny asked nervously.

"Then we'll have to confront Patricia with what we do have," I said, tapping Abigail's notebook. "Maybe it will be enough to make her slip up."

Margaret rose with surprising agility for a woman her age. "I'm coming with you. I know every nook and cranny of that community center, and as head of the gardening club, no one will question my presence there before the festival."

I hesitated, concerned about involving her further. "It could be dangerous."

Her laugh was dry as autumn leaves. "My dear, I'm seventy-two years old. Danger and I are old acquaintances. Besides," she added with a gleam in her eye, "I've been waiting decades to see Patricia Wilson get her comeuppance."

***

The community center was ablaze with lights when we arrived, cars filling the small parking lot as council members and committee heads gathered for the emergency meeting. We slipped in through a side entrance that Margaret assured us was rarely used, finding ourselves in a narrow hallway lined with storage closets.

"The Easter festival supplies are kept in the large storage room at the end of this hall," Margaret whispered, leading the way. "The egg hunt materials should be on shelves labeled 'Children's Activities.'"

We moved as quietly as possible, though the murmur of voices from the main meeting room covered most of our footsteps. Through a crack in the door as we passed, I caught a glimpse of Patricia Wilson standing at a podium, her silver hair gleaming under the fluorescent lights as she addressed the assembled town officials. She appeared perfectly composed, not at all like someone who had committed murder or who was actively trying to eliminate witnesses.

The storage room was unlocked, presumably because volunteers had been in and out all day preparing for the festival. Inside, shelves laden with colorful decorations, craft supplies, and boxes labeled for various activities lined the walls. Margaret headed straight for a section marked "Easter Egg Hunt" while Bunny and I began systematically searching through containers of plastic eggs, baskets, and bunny-shaped signs.

"Everything looks normal," Bunny whispered after several minutes of searching. "Just regular Easter stuff."

"We need to think like Abigail," I reasoned. "She was clever and methodical. Where would she hide something important but accessible?"

Margaret was examining a large basket filled with special prize eggs—larger, more decorative eggs that contained small toys or certificates for bigger prizes. "These premium eggs are distributed by committee members during the hunt," she explained. "Each one is numbered and assigned to a specific location."

Something about that tickled my memory. "Wait ... the notebook mentioned an 'Easter flash drive.' What if it's not hidden inside an egg, but disguised as one of these premium eggs?"

We began carefully examining each prize egg, checking for anything unusual. It was Bunny who found it—a slightly heavier egg with a small, almost imperceptible seam around its middle.

"This one feels different," she said, holding up a metallic pink egg adorned with delicate spring flowers.

I took it from her, turning it carefully in my hands. When I applied gentle pressure and twisted, the egg separated into two halves, revealing a small USB drive nestled inside a hollowed compartment.

"This has to be it," I breathed. "Abigail's insurance policy."

"But we can't be sure until we look at what's on it," Margaret pointed out. "And we'll need a computer for that."

"There's one in the administrative office," I suggested. "We could—"

The storage room door swung open, cutting me off mid-sentence. I hastily closed the egg and slipped it into my pocket as Patricia Wilson stepped into the doorway, her expression changing from surprise to cold calculation in an instant.

"Well," she said smoothly, "this is unexpected. Margaret, I thought you were skipping tonight's meeting due to your ... concerns ... about the accelerated vote."

"I reconsidered," Margaret replied with remarkable calm. "After all, this project will affect the entire town. I should be present for such an important decision."

Patricia's gaze shifted to Bunny and me. "And you two. I was informed you were being taken to Clayton for your protection. How interesting to find you here instead."

"We had concerns about our police escort," I said, matching her calm tone while my heart hammered in my chest. "Especially after receiving a threatening chocolate bunny at our shop."

"How terrifying for you," Patricia murmured, though her eyes remained cold. "All the more reason to be safely tucked away, rather than wandering around a storage room." Her gaze dropped to the boxes of Easter supplies. "Looking for something specific?"

"Just checking on the festival preparations," Margaret interjected. "Lee and Bunny kindly offered to help me organize the egg hunt materials."

"How considerate." Patricia stepped fully into the room, allowing the door to swing shut behind her. The click of the lock engaging was unnervingly loud in the sudden silence. "But I'm afraid the meeting is about to begin, and we have some rather pressing matters to discuss. Perhaps you could continue your . . . preparations . . . another time."

The metallic egg felt like it was burning a hole in my pocket. I needed to get it somewhere safe, somewhere I could access its contents before Patricia realized what we'd found.

"Of course," I agreed, moving toward the door. "We'll just get out of your way."

Patricia didn't budge from her position blocking the exit. "Actually, I'd like a private word with you first, Lee. About that threatening package you received. As head of the festival committee, I'm naturally concerned about any threats to our volunteers."

Her solicitous tone couldn't mask the danger in her eyes. She knew—or at least strongly suspected—that we'd found something incriminating.

"I've actually shared everything I know with Detective Morrison," I replied. "He's handling the investigation now."

"Detective Morrison has been called away to Clayton on an urgent matter," Patricia informed us with a thin smile. "Something about your aunt creating a disturbance at the hotel where she was supposed to be staying with you two."

My stomach dropped. If Aunt Nettie was causing a "disturbance," it was almost certainly because she'd realized Bunny and I were missing and was trying to alert Morrison to the danger we might be in.

"I really think we should join the meeting," Margaret said firmly, moving to stand beside me. "The entire council is waiting, Patricia."

"The council can wait a few more minutes," Patricia replied, reaching into her elegant handbag. When her hand emerged, it was holding something that glinted in the fluorescent lighting—a small, pearl-handled revolver. "I'm afraid we have a more urgent matter to resolve first."

Bunny let out a small gasp, instinctively stepping backward and colliding with a shelf of decorations. Several bunny-shaped signs clattered to the floor, but Patricia's attention never wavered.

"Patricia," Margaret said, her voice remarkably steady, "think about what you're doing. The entire town council is just down the hall."

"And they'll hear nothing over the ventilation system and their own chatter," Patricia responded confidently. "Besides, I've already prepared them for tragedy. A follow-up to the terrible events that claimed Abigail's life—three more victims of our mysterious Easter killer."

"You won't get away with this," I said, trying to keep her talking while my mind raced for a way out. "People already suspect you. Beau Birdsong has gone to the police with evidence of your involvement in Abigail's murder."

Something flickered in Patricia's eyes—uncertainty, perhaps? "Beau Birdsong is a desperate man trying to divert attention from his own complicity. He has nothing concrete."

"He has the partial download of Abigail's records," I countered. "Enough to show your conflict with her over the restoration project."

"A business disagreement isn't proof of murder," Patricia dismissed. "And any evidence he might have had will be tragically lost when his car goes off Miller's Bridge tonight during his drive back from the police station. Such dangerous curves on that road, especially when the guardrails haven't been properly maintained."

The casual way she referenced another planned murder chilled me to the bone. This woman had already killed once and was prepared to eliminate anyone who stood in her way without a moment's remorse.

"And what about this?" I pulled the metallic egg from my pocket, holding it up where she could see it clearly. "Abigail's insurance policy. Video evidence of you accessing the monkshood in the greenhouse the day she died."

For the first time, genuine alarm flashed across Patricia's composed features. "Give me that," she demanded, extending her free hand while keeping the revolver trained on us with the other.

"Why?" I challenged, emboldened by her reaction. "If you're innocent, this evidence won't harm you."

"Don't play games with me, Lee," Patricia's voice hardened. "That egg. Now."

I clutched it tighter. "If you shoot us, the noise will bring the entire council running, evidence or no evidence."

"Who said anything about shooting?" Patricia smiled coldly. "I have a much quieter method in mind." From her pocket, she produced a small chocolate bunny identical to the one left at our shop earlier. "A tragic case of accidental poisoning. Three festival volunteers sampling chocolate without realizing it contained a deadly allergen. By the time help arrives, it will be too late."

"No one would believe all three of us would eat suspicious chocolate, especially after what happened to Abigail," Margaret scoffed.

"Perhaps not voluntarily," Patricia conceded. "But with a gun persuading you? And afterward, I'll simply place the revolver in your hand, Margaret. You were always outspoken about your hatred for Abigail taking over your precious festival. Who's to say you didn't snap and murder her, then eliminate these two when they discovered your crime?"

It was a chillingly plausible scenario. Margaret's history with Abigail was well-known, and her name had been on the blackmail list. In the confusion following our deaths, Patricia could easily plant the gun and create a narrative that most people would accept, especially with her influence over the police chief.

"Now," Patricia continued, "the egg, Lee. Final warning."

I realized I had only one chance. Meeting Bunny's eyes briefly, I gave an almost imperceptible nod before turning back to Patricia.

"Fine," I said, holding out the metallic egg. "Take it."

As Patricia reached for it with her free hand, I deliberately fumbled, dropping the egg to the floor where it split open, the USB drive skittering under a nearby shelf. Patricia's gaze automatically followed it—and in that split second of distraction, Bunny did what she did best: created chaos.

With a tremendous crash, she pulled an entire shelf of Easter decorations down, sending baskets, plastic eggs, and bunny signs cascading across the floor. Margaret lunged forward with surprising agility, striking Patricia's arm and sending the revolver flying into the corner of the room.

I dove for the gun while Patricia scrambled for the USB drive, but before either of us could reach our targets, the storage room door burst open with a splintering crack. Detective Morrison stood in the doorway, his own weapon drawn.

"Nobody move!" he commanded, quickly assessing the scene before him.

Patricia froze halfway to the USB drive, then smoothly straightened up, composing her features into a mask of relief. "Detective! Thank goodness you're here. These women broke into the community center. When I confronted them, they became violent."

"That's not true!" Bunny protested. "She pulled a gun on us! She was going to poison us with chocolate, just like she did to Abigail!"

Morrison's gaze remained steady, giving away nothing as he surveyed the chaos of the storage room. "Mrs. Wilson, please step away from that USB drive on the floor."

Patricia's mask slipped slightly. "What USB drive? I don't see anything."

"The one you were reaching for just now," Morrison replied calmly. "The one that fell out of that broken egg." He nodded toward the metallic pink egg lying in two pieces on the floor.

Seeing that denial was futile, Patricia changed tactics. "This is all a misunderstanding. I was simply trying to secure potential evidence until you arrived. These women have been making wild accusations—"

"Save it for your statement, Mrs. Wilson," Morrison cut her off, nodding to two uniformed officers who had appeared behind him. "Officers, please secure the scene and collect that USB drive as evidence. And Mrs. Wilson's handbag as well—I believe we'll find a poisoned chocolate bunny inside."

As the officers moved to carry out his instructions, I stared at Morrison in confusion. "How did you know? I thought you were in Clayton dealing with my aunt."

"Your aunt is a very resourceful woman," he replied with the ghost of a smile. "Once she realized you two had given her escorts the slip, she created enough of a disturbance to ensure I'd be called personally. When I arrived at the hotel and found neither of you there, I put together a few pieces of the puzzle."

"Beau's statement," I guessed.

Morrison nodded. "That, and the fact that forensics found traces of monkshood in that chocolate bunny left at your shop.

The same poison used to kill Abigail Thornton, combined with concentrated peanut oil to trigger her allergy. Very distinctive."

Patricia maintained her composure even as the officers carefully bagged the evidence and placed handcuffs on her wrists. "This is ridiculous. I'm the mayor's wife. I'm chairperson of five community committees. I don't go around poisoning people with chocolate rabbits."

"Actually, Mrs. Wilson," Morrison countered, holding up a clear evidence bag containing the USB drive, "we'll let the contents of this decide that. And the surveillance footage from the community center showing you entering this storage room with a revolver in your hand ten minutes ago."

Her face finally crumpled, the careful mask of civic leadership giving way to cold fury. "You have no idea what you're dealing with," she hissed. "Half the town is implicated in Abigail's schemes. Do you really think they'll let you pursue this? Chief Parker—"

"—has recused himself from this investigation," Morrison finished for her. "Apparently, your late-night call informing him of a 'situation' that needed handling at the Clayton hotel was enough to make him question where his loyalties should lie. Especially when I mentioned potential charges of conspiracy and evidence tampering."

As the officers led Patricia away, her final venomous glare fell on me. "This isn't over, Lee Woodyard. Sweetwater Springs has secrets you couldn't begin to imagine."

The threat hung in the air even after she was gone, a chilling reminder of the tangled web of influence and blackmail that had nearly consumed our town.

"Is it really over?" Bunny asked quietly, surveying the destroyed storage room.

"The immediate danger is," Morrison assured her. "Mrs. Wilson will be formally charged with the murder of Abigail Thornton, as well as attempted murder of the three of you. And with the evidence on that USB drive, I suspect we'll have a very solid case."

"What about the town council meeting?" Margaret asked, straightening her cardigan with dignity despite the chaos around us. "Patricia was about to force through the vote on the restoration project."

"I think that vote will be postponed indefinitely once the council members learn of tonight's events," Morrison replied. "And from what I understand of Mr. Birdsong's statement, several of them may have their own explaining to do regarding their roles in Abigail's blackmail schemes."

The mention of Beau jolted me. "Is he safe? Patricia said something about his car going off Miller's Bridge tonight."

"Mr. Birdsong is in protective custody," Morrison assured me. "Though I'll alert the department to keep an eye on that bridge, just in case Mrs. Wilson had arranged something before her arrest."

A wave of exhaustion suddenly washed over me as the adrenaline began to fade. The past two days had been a whirlwind of murder, blackmail, and narrow escapes—a far cry from the chocolate bunnies and Easter festivals that usually occupied my April.

"Can we go home now?" I asked wearily. "I need to call my aunt and let her know we're alright."

Morrison nodded. "I'll need formal statements from all of you tomorrow, but for tonight, yes, you can go home. I'll have officers escort you, and there will be a patrol car outside your residence overnight—real protection this time, I promise."

As we made our way through the community center, past the stunned faces of council members who had gathered for a vote and were instead witnessing the arrest of the mayor's wife, I couldn't help but wonder how Sweetwater Springs would recover from this Easter season's bitter revelations. The restoration project, Abigail's blackmail schemes, Patricia's murder—these would leave scars on our small town that wouldn't heal quickly.

But as we stepped outside into the cool spring night, with the Easter decorations gently swaying in the breeze and the first stars appearing overhead, I felt a glimmer of hope. Tomorrow was Good Friday, the beginning of Easter weekend proper. A time of renewal and fresh starts.

And despite everything, I found myself smiling at the thought of creating chocolate delights for the children of Sweetwater Springs—normalcy returning like the sweet aftertaste that lingers after a perfect piece of chocolate.

"What are you smiling about?" Bunny asked as we waited for our police escort.

"I was just thinking that we still have hundreds of Easter orders to fill," I replied. "And for once, I'm actually looking forward to it."

Margaret chuckled softly. "After facing down a murderer with a gun, I imagine piping chocolate bunnies seems rather straightforward."

"Exactly," I agreed. "And you know what? I think this year, I might finally appreciate the true meaning of Easter—new beginnings rising from darkness. Sweetwater Springs is going to need that renewal now more than ever."

As a police cruiser pulled up to take us home, I took one last look at the community center, where Detective Morrison was speaking intently with the mayor. Frank Wilson's round face looked deflated, the shock of his wife's arrest and the revelation of her crimes clearly overwhelming him.

"New beginnings for everyone," I murmured, before sliding into the back seat beside Bunny. "Even if some are harder than others."

***

By the time we reached my Victorian house, the news of Patricia Wilson's arrest had already spread through town with the lightning speed that only small-town gossip networks can achieve. My phone had exploded with messages from concerned customers, curious neighbors, and most urgently, Aunt Nettie, who had apparently been giving the hotel staff in Clayton fits with her demands to know where her niece and employee had disappeared to.

As promised, Morrison had arranged for a patrol car to remain outside overnight, though I suspected the danger had passed with Patricia's arrest. Inside, Bunny made hot chocolate while I called Aunt Nettie, reassuring her that we were safe and filling her in on the evening's dramatic events.

"I'll be home first thing in the morning," she declared once her immediate concerns were satisfied. "Detective Morrison is sending an officer to drive me back tonight, but I insisted on staying to give my statement first. Someone in this family should follow proper procedure." The affectionate exasperation in her voice made me smile.

"We'll be waiting with fresh cinnamon rolls," I promised.

"And explanations," she added pointedly. "Full explanations."

After hanging up, I joined Bunny in the kitchen, where she had set out mugs of hot chocolate topped with homemade marshmallows—a specialty she had mastered during her short time at Heavenly Confections.

"I still can't believe it's over," she said, her hands wrapped around her mug for warmth. "Everything happened so fast—Abigail's murder, the investigation, Patricia's arrest... it's been less than forty-eight hours."

"The fastest forty-eight hours of my life," I agreed, sinking into a chair at the kitchen table. "Though I have a feeling the aftermath will last considerably longer."

Bunny nodded solemnly. "What happens now? To the shop? To the town?"

"We go back to making chocolates," I said simply. "We fill our Easter orders, we participate in the festival, we move forward. The restoration project will probably be abandoned or completely redesigned without Abigail and Patricia pushing it through. Mr. Jenkins assured us our building is safe, and I suspect many other property owners will be equally relieved to be free of the pressure to sell."

"And Beau?" she asked, her voice smaller. "What happens with him?"

I studied her carefully. Despite everything her estranged husband had done—the blackmail, the deception, the theft of our storage key—there was still a vulnerability in her eyes when she spoke his name.

"That depends on Detective Morrison," I replied gently. "Beau's cooperation will probably earn him some leniency, but he was still involved in Abigail's blackmail schemes. There will be consequences."

Bunny nodded, her expression a mixture of sadness and resolution. "I think... I think I'm finally ready to move on. For real this time. Whatever happens with the divorce, with his legal troubles... I need to focus on my own future."

"At Heavenly Confections?" I suggested.

A smile broke through her melancholy. "If you'll still have me. I promise to try very hard not to drop any more chocolate molds."

"Are you kidding? After the way you handled yourself tonight? Bunny, you saved our lives with that well-timed shelf collapse. I'd say that more than makes up for a few broken molds."

Her cheeks flushed with pleasure at the praise. "Really? I was just doing what comes naturally—creating chaos."

"Sometimes chaos is exactly what's needed," I told her with a laugh. "And speaking of chaos, we have about three hundred Easter orders to fill tomorrow. We should probably get some sleep."

As I showed Bunny to the guest room and prepared for bed myself, I found my thoughts drifting to Detective Morrison. His timely arrival at the community center had saved our lives, and throughout the investigation, he had shown a commitment to the truth that impressed me, especially in a town so tangled with secrets and influence.

Perhaps once the Easter rush was over, I'd invite him for coffee. Professional curiosity, of course—to discuss the resolution of the case. Nothing more than that.

With that thought warming me more than it probably should, I drifted off to sleep, dreaming not of murder and blackmail, but of chocolate bunnies and fresh beginnings in a town slowly healing from its darkest secrets.

The final bite of this Easter mystery had been bitter indeed, but the sweetness of justice—and perhaps new friendship—lingered like the perfect chocolate finish.

Chapter 7: Sweet Justice

Easter Sunday dawned bright and clear, as if the weather itself was celebrating the renewed spirit of Sweetwater Springs. The past three days had been a whirlwind of activity—equal parts chocolate-making marathon and community recovery.

The Easter festival had proceeded as planned, albeit with some hasty reorganization after Patricia Wilson's arrest. Margaret Wilkins had stepped back into her long-held role as committee chairperson with remarkable efficiency, and the town square had transformed into the pastel wonderland that residents looked forward to each spring.

Saturday's egg hunt had been a particular success, with children racing across the green to find colorful treasures while their parents chatted about recent events in hushed, excited tones. The general consensus seemed to be shock mingled with a strange sense of relief—as if a weight had been lifted from the town without most people having realized it was there in the first place.

Now, standing behind the counter at Heavenly Confections, I surveyed our handiwork with exhausted satisfaction. The shop gleamed, every surface polished to perfection. Display cases were filled with our finest Easter creations—artisanal chocolate bunnies, hand-painted eggs, and specialty confections that had taken the better part of two sleepless nights to complete.

"I think we've outdone ourselves this year," Aunt Nettie declared, adjusting a basket of truffle-filled eggs. "Though I suppose nothing increases productivity quite like recovering from an attempt on your life."

"Aunt Nettie!" I protested, though I couldn't help but smile at her characteristic bluntness.

"What? It's true." She patted my cheek affectionately. "Nothing clarifies priorities like nearly being poisoned by the mayor's wife."

Before I could respond, the bell above the door jingled cheerfully as Bunny bustled in, her arms laden with fresh flowers for our Easter display. Her platinum blonde hair was adorned with a small butterfly clip, and she wore a spring dress so colorful it rivaled our Easter decorations.

"Sorry I'm late!" she exclaimed, carefully setting down her floral burden. "Mrs. Henderson stopped me on the way to ask for all the 'insider details' about Patricia's arrest. That woman is relentless."

"And what did you tell her?" I asked, helping her arrange the flowers around our featured display.

Bunny's expression turned uncharacteristically mischievous. "That I'd signed an exclusive deal with a true crime podcast and couldn't possibly comment."

Aunt Nettie laughed in delight. "Bunny Birdsong, I do believe you're developing a backbone. I heartily approve."

The past few days had indeed revealed unexpected depths to our newest employee. Since the confrontation at the community center, Bunny had shown a quiet determination that belied her typically scattered demeanor. She'd thrown herself into the Easter preparations with focused energy, mastering decorative techniques that had previously eluded her and dropping significantly fewer trays in the process.

"Detective Morrison called this morning," I mentioned as we put the finishing touches on the display. "Patricia Wilson is being formally charged today. Murder in the first degree for Abigail, attempted murder for the three of us, plus conspiracy, blackmail, and a host of other charges."

"Will it stick?" Bunny asked, voicing the concern that had been nagging at me.

"Morrison thinks so. The evidence on that USB drive was damning—clear footage of Patricia accessing the monkshood in the greenhouse, plus financial records detailing the entire scheme." I arranged a chocolate bunny at a more appealing angle. "And Beau's testimony is apparently quite comprehensive."

The mention of Beau caused a flicker of emotion across Bunny's face—not pain exactly, but something more complex. She had visited him once in police custody, emerging from the brief meeting with quiet resolve and signing the divorce papers he had finally agreed to without conditions.

"What about the mayor?" Aunt Nettie inquired. "Any charges for Frank?"

I shook my head. "Apparently, he was largely in the dark about the extent of Patricia's activities. Morrison says he was more of a figurehead than a co-conspirator. He's resigned as mayor, effective immediately. The town council will appoint an interim replacement until a special election can be held."

"Poor Frank," Aunt Nettie murmured, though without much conviction. "Always suspected he was more puppet than politician."

The morning passed in a blur of customers, many stopping by as much for gossip as for chocolate. We maintained a unified approach—acknowledging the events without embellishment, focusing conversations back on our Easter offerings, and gently steering clear of speculation about ongoing legal proceedings.

By noon, we had sold through nearly half our Easter stock, and I found myself mentally calculating whether our supplies would last through the day. Aunt Nettie had just flipped the "Open" sign to "Closed for Lunch" when the bell jangled once more.

"We're closed for—" I began automatically, then stopped when I saw Detective Morrison standing awkwardly in the doorway, holding what appeared to be a small potted plant.

"Sorry," he said, already backing toward the exit. "I can come back later."

"No, no," Aunt Nettie insisted, waving him in. "We're just closed to the general chocolate-crazed public. Law enforcement is always welcome, especially when bearing gifts."

Morrison stepped inside, the ghost of a smile playing at his lips. He was dressed casually today in jeans and a button-down shirt rather than his usual professional attire. The change suited him.

"It's an Easter lily," he explained, offering the plant to me. "Traditional this time of year. And a small thank you for your help with the case."

I accepted it with a warmth that couldn't be entirely attributed to professional courtesy. "That's very thoughtful. Though I'm pretty sure you're the one who saved us, not the other way around."

"It was a collaborative effort," he replied diplomatically. "The evidence you three uncovered was instrumental in building our case against Mrs. Wilson."

"How is that going?" Aunt Nettie asked, gesturing for him to join us at one of the small café tables we'd set up for the Easter weekend chocolate tastings.

Morrison settled into a chair with a sigh that spoke volumes about his recent workload. "Complicated, but progressing. Patricia Wilson had her fingers in many pies, as they say. We're still unraveling all the connections."

"And Chief Parker?" I asked.

"Suspended pending investigation," Morrison confirmed. "He maintains he was unaware of the murder plot, though he admits to helping cover up his son's legal troubles years ago. The county sheriff's department has taken over operations temporarily."

Bunny emerged from the kitchen with a tray of samples we'd prepared for the afternoon tasting. Seeing Morrison, she almost dropped the tray—old habits die hard—but managed to recover with only a slight wobble.

"Detective!" she exclaimed. "Would you like to try our new Easter truffle assortment? I created the raspberry ganache filling myself."

"I'd be honored," he replied with a warmth that made Bunny beam with pride.

As she arranged the samples on the table, the bell jangled again. This time it was Margaret Wilkins, immaculately dressed as always, though today she'd added a festive pastel scarf to her usual practical attire.

"I hope I'm not interrupting," she said, surveying our little gathering. "I wanted to drop off the final schedule for today's Easter festival closing ceremony. And," she added with unusual hesitation, "to invite you all to a small get-together at my home afterward. A celebration of sorts."

"Celebration of Easter or of Patricia's arrest?" Aunt Nettie asked with characteristic directness.

Margaret's lips twitched. "Can't it be both? It's been a trying week for our community. I thought a modest gathering of those who understand the full picture might be . . . restorative."

"Count us in," I assured her. "Though we'll need to close the shop first."

"Of course. Seven o'clock." She turned to Morrison. "Detective, you're included in this invitation. Your work has not gone unnoticed or unappreciated."

He looked surprised but pleased. "Thank you, Mrs. Wilkins. I'll be there."

After Margaret departed, we fell into a surprisingly comfortable conversation about the festival, the shop, and the general rhythms of life in Sweetwater Springs. Morrison—James, as he invited us to call him—proved to be thoughtful and dry-witted when not in his official capacity. I found myself watching the way his eyes crinkled when he smiled, the careful way he considered each chocolate truffle before tasting it.

"These are extraordinary," he declared after sampling Bunny's raspberry creation. "You have a genuine talent, Ms. Birdsong."

Bunny flushed with pleasure. "Thank you! I've been experimenting with flavor combinations. Lee has been teaching me the finer points of ganache consistency."

"She's a quick study," I added. "We're thinking of featuring a 'Bunny's Choice' truffle selection for the summer season."

"You're keeping me?" Bunny asked, her eyes widening. "I mean, as a permanent employee? Even after all the . . . chaos?"

Aunt Nettie laughed. "My dear, after what we've been through together, you're practically family. Besides, your natural disaster tendencies seem to be improving daily."

"Speaking of improvements," Morrison said, turning to me, "I wanted to let you know that Mr. Jenkins has filed for permits to make some modest updates to your building. Nothing like what the restoration project envisioned—just structural maintenance and some modernized features he's been putting off."

"He mentioned something about that yesterday," I nodded. "Said he'd been inspired to 'invest in what matters' after his brush with Abigail's schemes."

"Many people seem to be reassessing priorities," Morrison observed. "The interim mayor—Harold Finch from the hardware store—has already announced plans to review all recent zoning changes and property transactions for irregularities."

"Cleaning house," Aunt Nettie said approvingly. "Long overdue, if you ask me."

After Morrison left—with a promise to see us at Margaret's gathering that evening—we reopened the shop for the afternoon rush. Customers flowed in steadily, many dressed in their Easter finery straight from church services, eager to pick up last-minute treats for family celebrations.

Mr. Jenkins stopped by, looking more like his old dapper self in a pastel blue suit with a matching pocket square. "Just wanted to say happy Easter to my favorite tenants," he announced, presenting us each with a small potted hyacinth. "And to confirm that your lease remains unchanged for as long as you wish to stay."

"That's very generous," Aunt Nettie said, genuinely touched. "We've always been happy here."

"As you should be," he replied firmly. "Some things don't need 'revitalization' or 'modernizing' to have value. Some things are perfect just as they are." With a tip of his hat, he was gone, leaving behind the sweet scent of spring flowers.

The afternoon passed in a pleasant blur of sales and conversations. By closing time, our cases were nearly empty, with only a few chocolate bunnies and assorted truffles remaining.

"Record sales," Aunt Nettie declared happily as she tallied the day's receipts. "Despite murder, blackmail, and general mayhem. Perhaps we should have a crisis every Easter."

"Please, no," I groaned, though I couldn't help but smile at her irrepressible spirit. "One murderous chocolate bunny per lifetime is more than enough."

Bunny, who was carefully packing our remaining inventory for donation to the children's hospital in Clayton, looked up with unexpected seriousness. "Do you think it's really over? All the secrets and schemes?"

I considered her question as I wiped down the counter. "Some of it, yes. Patricia is facing serious charges, the restoration project has been suspended indefinitely, and several council members have suddenly discovered urgent needs to spend time with family out of state."

"But the underlying system. . ." Aunt Nettie mused, setting aside the cash register tape. "The influence, the favors, the quiet arrangements that have governed this town for generations—those don't disappear overnight."

"No," I agreed. "But they've been exposed to sunlight, and that's a powerful disinfectant. People are talking openly about things that were only whispered before. That's a start."

"A new beginning," Bunny suggested. "Like Easter is supposed to be."

"Exactly." I smiled at her unexpected insight. "Speaking of which, we should finish up here if we're going to make it to Margaret's gathering."

***

Margaret Wilkins's home was exactly what you'd expect from Sweetwater Springs' premier gardener—a charming cottage surrounded by meticulously maintained flower beds that somehow managed to be both perfectly ordered and naturally beautiful. Inside, the decor was elegant but comfortable, with fresh flowers adorning every surface.

To my surprise, Detective Morrison—James—was already there when we arrived, engaged in what appeared to be an animated conversation with Margaret about native plant species. He greeted us warmly, his eyes lingering on mine just long enough to send a pleasant flutter through my chest.

The small gathering included a select group: Mr. Jenkins; Harold Finch, our interim mayor; Reverend Thomas from the First Baptist Church; and to my shock, Beau Birdsong, looking subdued in simple khakis and a button-down rather than his usual designer attire.

Bunny faltered slightly at the sight of her soon-to-be-ex-husband, but squared her shoulders and nodded politely in his direction before deliberately engaging Reverend Thomas in conversation about the children's Easter program. I couldn't help but admire her composure.

"He requested permission to attend," James murmured, appearing at my elbow with a glass of wine. "Part of his cooperation agreement allows limited social engagements. I hope it's not uncomfortable for you."

"Not for me," I replied, accepting the wine gratefully. "But Bunny—"

"Seems to be handling it admirably," he finished, nodding toward where she was now laughing at something the reverend had said. "She's stronger than she appears."

"We've all discovered hidden strengths lately," I agreed, thinking of my own confrontation with Patricia. "Though I'd prefer less dramatic methods of self-discovery in the future."

James smiled, the expression warming his usually serious features. "Noted. I'll try to keep murderous conspiracies to a minimum in Sweetwater Springs going forward."

"See that you do, Detective," I teased. "Our insurance doesn't cover 'death by chocolate' incidents."

Margaret called for our attention then, gathering everyone in her comfortable living room. Once we were settled, she raised her glass in a toast.

"To Sweetwater Springs," she began, her voice clear and strong despite her years. "A town that has weathered many storms, including this recent tempest of corruption and deceit. But also to truth, which like the spring flowers, eventually finds its way to the light."

"To truth," we echoed, glasses raised.

"And to new beginnings," she continued. "Which seems appropriate on this Easter Sunday. Our community has been granted a chance to start fresh, to rebuild on a foundation of transparency rather than secrets."

Harold Finch, a stocky man with perpetually paint-stained hands from his hardware store, cleared his throat. "As interim mayor, I want to assure everyone that the town council will be operating with complete openness moving forward. All meetings will be public, all records accessible, all decisions made in the clear light of day."

"A welcome change," Mr. Jenkins commented, raising his glass again.

I noticed that Beau remained quiet throughout these exchanges, his expression thoughtful rather than his usual confident mask. When he caught me watching him, he gave a small, almost apologetic nod before returning his attention to Margaret.

"There is one more order of business," she announced. "Detective Morrison has requested a moment to share some news regarding the ongoing investigation."

James set down his glass and moved to the center of the room. "Thank you for allowing me to intrude on your celebration. I wanted to inform those most directly affected by recent events that we've made significant progress in unraveling the full extent of Abigail Thornton and Patricia Wilson's network."

He outlined how the evidence from Abigail's USB drive, combined with files recovered from Patricia's home computer and Beau's testimony, had exposed a web of manipulation extending back nearly a decade. Several prominent business owners in neighboring towns had been implicated in financial improprieties. Three county officials had resigned rather than face investigation.

"The most significant development," James continued, "is that we've uncovered the identity of Abigail's mysterious partner—the financial backer who provided capital for her various schemes, including the restoration project."

I leaned forward, surprised. Neither Beau nor Patricia had mentioned an outside investor in their confessions.

"A real estate developer from Chicago named Victor Markham," James revealed. "He's been buying up properties in small towns across three states, using local frontpeople like Abigail to mask his activities. The FBI has had him under investigation for months, and our evidence has provided the missing links they needed."

"So Abigail was just another pawn?" Aunt Nettie asked, incredulous.

"A particularly effective one," James clarified. "But yes, ultimately she was executing someone else's vision—though with her own ambitious twist."

"And this Markham person," I asked, "he's being charged as well?"

James nodded. "Arrested this morning in Chicago. Which means the threat to Sweetwater Springs is truly neutralized—not just the local operators, but the source of the scheme itself."

A collective sigh of relief seemed to flow through the room. It was one thing to know that Patricia was in custody; it was another to learn that the shadow hanging over our town had been completely dispelled.

After James finished his update, the gathering took on a more celebratory tone. Margaret served a delicious Easter dinner, complete with traditional ham, scalloped potatoes, and fresh spring vegetables from her own garden. Conversation flowed easily, jumping from town business to festival highlights to cautiously optimistic plans for the future.

I found myself seated between James and Beau during dinner, an awkward arrangement that proved unexpectedly illuminating. Beau, stripped of his usual arrogance, spoke candidly about his involvement in Abigail's schemes and his regret over the damage caused.

"I convinced myself it was just business," he admitted quietly as we finished our meal. "That no one was really getting hurt. Just property changing hands, development moving forward— progress, or so I thought."

"And now?" I asked, curious despite my lingering anger toward him.

He glanced across the table at Bunny, who was deep in conversation with Aunt Nettie and Margaret. "Now I understand what actually matters. Too late, perhaps, but still." He turned back to me. "I know you don't have any reason to believe this, but I am truly sorry for my part in all of this. Especially for taking that key from your shop—involving you and your aunt in a situation that could have ended much worse."

Before I could respond, James spoke up. "Your cooperation has been noted in my reports, Mr. Birdsong. It will likely factor favorably in your sentencing."

Beau nodded acknowledgment. "I appreciate that, Detective. But I'm not cooperating for a reduced sentence. Some debts can't be paid with legal maneuvering."

As dinner concluded and we moved to Margaret's sunroom for coffee and dessert—a selection of Heavenly Confections chocolates we'd brought as our contribution—I found myself standing beside James, watching the sunset paint the garden in golden light.

"Beautiful, isn't it?" he commented, nodding toward the riotous display of spring flowers. "Hard to believe so much was happening beneath this peaceful surface."

"Small towns are like that," I replied. "Still waters often run deep—and sometimes murky."

"And now? Do you think Sweetwater Springs can recover its tranquility without the murkiness?"

I considered his question, watching as Aunt Nettie regaled the group with a story that had everyone laughing, even the subdued Beau. "I think we have a chance. Not to pretend the darkness never existed, but to acknowledge it and choose a different path forward."

"Very philosophical," James observed with a small smile. "And what about you? What path are you choosing?"

The question carried weight beyond its simple phrasing. I turned to face him fully, taking in his genuine interest, the warm intelligence in his eyes.

"I'm choosing to stay right here," I said. "Making chocolate, building Heavenly Confections, being part of this community as it heals and grows. And maybe. . ." I hesitated, then continued with newfound boldness, "maybe exploring some new possibilities along the way."

"New possibilities," he repeated thoughtfully. "I like the sound of that."

Before he could elaborate, Bunny appeared with a tray of our signature truffles. "Dessert is served! I recommend the dark chocolate lavender—it pairs beautifully with Margaret's coffee."

The moment shifted back to the social gathering, but something had changed—a door had opened to future conversations, future possibilities.

As the evening wound down and we prepared to leave, Margaret pulled me aside. "You did well," she said simply. "Abigail would never have expected such formidable opposition from a chocolate shop owner."

"I'm learning not to underestimate anyone in this town," I replied. "Especially not its gardening club president."

She laughed, the sound unexpectedly youthful. "We all have our secrets, Lee. The difference is in how we use them." She patted my hand. "I think Sweetwater Springs is in good hands moving forward. Between your aunt's wisdom, your determination, and even young Bunny's surprising resilience . . . not to mention our new detective's integrity."

"Speaking of whom," I said, noticing James gathering his coat. "I should say goodnight."

Margaret's knowing smile told me she understood exactly what remained unspoken.

Outside in the cool evening air, James offered to walk us to our car. Aunt Nettie, displaying unusual tact, suddenly remembered something she needed to discuss with Margaret and ducked back inside, pulling Bunny along with her despite the younger woman's confused protests.

"Subtle," James commented dryly as they disappeared.

"About as subtle as one of Bunny's kitchen accidents," I agreed with a laugh.

We stood in comfortable silence for a moment, the Easter moon rising full and bright above Margaret's flower beds. All across Sweetwater Springs, families were concluding their holiday celebrations, dishes being washed, children being tucked into bed after sugar-fueled excitement.

"I was thinking," James said finally, "once things settle down a bit with the investigation, maybe we could have dinner sometime. Not to discuss the case," he added quickly.

"I'd like that," I replied, surprised by how much I meant it. After my divorce from Richard, I'd thrown myself into the chocolate shop, convinced that romance was a complication I could live without. But something about James Morrison—his steadiness, his quiet integrity during the chaos of the past few days—had slipped past my defenses.

"Good," he said simply. "It's a date, then."

The word "date" hung in the air between us, full of possibility. Before either of us could elaborate, Aunt Nettie and Bunny emerged from the house, their timing too perfect to be coincidental.

"Ready to go, Lee?" Aunt Nettie asked with exaggerated innocence. "We have an early start tomorrow with all those special orders to fill."

"Yes, we should get going," I agreed, though reluctantly. "Thank you again for the Easter lily, Detective. . . James. And for everything else."

"Just doing my job," he replied, though his smile suggested otherwise. "Though I admit, this has been the most interesting case of my career. Not every investigation ends with me being invited to Easter dinner."

"Let's hope your next case is significantly less dramatic," I said.

"But not too boring," he countered, his eyes meeting mine with warmth that had nothing to do with professional courtesy.

As we drove home through the quiet streets of Sweetwater Springs, Bunny dozed in the backseat while Aunt Nettie hummed softly along with the radio. The town looked peaceful under the Easter moon, holiday decorations glowing gently in windows and on porches.

"Quite a weekend," Aunt Nettie observed, breaking the comfortable silence. "Murder, blackmail, corporate conspiracy, and a potential romance with the detective. Not bad for our little chocolate shop."

"Aunt Nettie!" I protested, feeling warmth creep into my cheeks.

"Oh please," she scoffed good-naturedly. "I may be old, but I'm not blind. That man looks at you the way someone examines a particularly exquisite truffle—appreciative and eager for a taste."

"That's a terrible analogy," I groaned, though I couldn't help laughing.

"But accurate," she insisted. "And I approve, for what it's worth. He has integrity. That's rare these days."

Coming from Aunt Nettie, this was high praise indeed. I found myself smiling as we pulled into our driveway, the Victorian house welcoming us home with warm lights we'd left on earlier.

Later, as I prepared for bed, I found myself reflecting on the extraordinary chain of events that had begun with a half-eaten chocolate bunny clutched in Abigail Thornton's lifeless hand.

What had started as a threat to our business—and later to our lives—had ultimately cleared away long-festering corruption and opened doors to unexpected new beginnings.

For Bunny, a chance to truly start fresh, freed from both Beau's manipulation and the shadow of suspicion. For Sweetwater Springs, an opportunity to rebuild its governance with transparency and integrity. For me, perhaps, a new chapter that included more than just chocolate-making in my future.

As I drifted toward sleep, I found myself looking forward to tomorrow's work with renewed purpose. Easter was officially over, but its message of renewal seemed more relevant than ever. Like the perfect chocolate, life was offering a complex blend of bitter and sweet—and I was finally ready to savor every flavor.

***

Monday morning dawned with the refreshed energy that always follows a holiday. The shop remained closed for our traditional post-Easter recovery day, but I was up early nonetheless, drawn to the kitchen by both habit and inspiration.

Aunt Nettie found me there, experimenting with a new truffle recipe—dark chocolate infused with lavender and honey, a combination I'd been contemplating for weeks but hadn't found time to perfect.

"Inspired, are we?" she observed, eyeing the neat rows of ganache-filled shells cooling on the marble slab.

"Just thinking ahead to summer," I replied, carefully tempering a batch of white chocolate for decorative drizzles. "Lavender will be in bloom soon."

"Mmm-hmm," she hummed skeptically, helping herself to a sample. "And would these happen to be for a certain detective with a newly discovered appreciation for fine chocolates?"

Before I could formulate a suitably dignified response, there was a knock at the back door. Bunny stood on the porch, her arms filled with newspapers.

"Have you seen these?" she asked breathlessly as Aunt Nettie let her in. "We're on the front page of every paper in the county!"

She spread them across the kitchen table: The Sweetwater Gazette, The Clayton Chronicle, even The Millfield Reporter. All featured variations of the same headline: "EASTER MURDER PLOT FOILED" or "MAYOR'S WIFE ARRESTED IN CHOCOLATE CONSPIRACY."

"Well," Aunt Nettie said dryly, examining the somewhat sensationalized accounts of our adventure, "I suppose this is one way to get publicity for the shop. Though I'm not sure 'Chocolates To Die For' is quite the slogan we were aiming for."

Despite her joke, I could see the concern behind her eyes. Would our business forever be associated with murder and poisoned chocolate bunnies? Would customers hesitate to buy our creations, wondering if another Patricia Wilson lurked in the shadows?

As if reading my thoughts, Bunny pulled out her phone. "I've been checking our online orders this morning," she said, bringing up the shop's website. "We've received twenty-seven new orders since yesterday evening. Most with notes saying they read about us in the papers and want to support 'the brave chocolate ladies who caught a killer.'"

I couldn't help but laugh at the dramatic description. "Brave chocolate ladies? Is that our new brand identity?"

"Could be worse," Aunt Nettie pointed out. "And it seems to be good for business."

The ringing of the doorbell interrupted our impromptu marketing discussion. Through the kitchen door, I could see James

Morrison standing on our front porch, once again holding something in his hands—this time what appeared to be a folder rather than a plant.

"Delivery for you," Aunt Nettie announced unnecessarily, ushering him into the kitchen with a knowing smile that made me want to disappear into the pantry.

"Sorry to intrude on your day off," James said, looking a bit more official today in his detective attire. "But I thought you'd want to see this as soon as possible." He placed the folder on the table. "The preliminary report on the chocolate bunny left at your shop. It was indeed poisoned with the same substances that killed Abigail Thornton."

"So Patricia really was planning to eliminate all of us," Bunny murmured, unconsciously touching her throat.

James nodded grimly. "The dosage was even higher than what was used on Abigail. She wasn't taking any chances."

"But all's well that ends well, right?" Aunt Nettie said briskly, reaching for the coffee pot. "Coffee, Detective? And perhaps one of Lee's experimental new truffles? She's been very . . . creative . . . this morning."

I shot her a look that promised retribution, but James accepted both offers with a smile that suggested he wasn't entirely unaware of her matchmaking efforts.

"I also wanted to let you know," he continued after sampling a truffle with appreciative noises that did nothing for my composure, "that the Easter flash drive contained more than just evidence against Patricia. It had comprehensive documentation of all of Abigail's schemes, including her connection to Victor Markham and their plans for several other small towns in the region."

"So this went beyond just Sweetwater Springs," I mused, sobered by the thought of other communities facing similar threats.

"Much bigger," James confirmed. "The FBI is calling it one of the most sophisticated real estate fraud schemes they've encountered. They've already issued warnings to several towns that were on Markham's target list."

"All because of a chocolate bunny with a USB drive inside," Bunny said wonderingly.

"And three very determined women who refused to be intimidated," James added, his gaze lingering on me.

Aunt Nettie, displaying unusual tact for the second time in twenty-four hours, suddenly remembered an urgent need to check inventory in the shop, dragging a protesting Bunny along with her and leaving James and me alone in the kitchen.

"Your aunt is about as subtle as a sledgehammer," he observed with amusement.

"Family trait," I admitted. "We Woodyard women tend to go directly for what we want."

"Is that so?" He set down his coffee cup, his expression turning more serious. "And what is it you want, Lee Woodyard, now that the murder is solved and the shop is safe?"

The question hung between us, weighted with possibilities. A week ago, my answer would have been simple: to run Heavenly Confections in peace, to create beautiful chocolates, to live quietly in the town I loved. But the events of the past few days had awakened something in me—a desire for more, for connection beyond the comfortable routines I'd established.

"I'm still figuring that out," I answered honestly. "But I think it might include dinner with a certain detective. Perhaps this weekend?"

His smile was answer enough, but he added, "I was hoping you'd say that. Saturday at seven? There's a new restaurant in Clayton that's supposed to be excellent."

"It's a date," I confirmed, echoing his words from the previous evening.

After James left—with a promise to call later in the week to finalize details—I returned to my chocolate-making with renewed focus. The truffle shells had set perfectly, ready for their ganache centers and decorative flourishes.

Aunt Nettie and Bunny returned from their tactical retreat, both pretending not to notice my slightly flushed cheeks or the extra care I was suddenly taking with the lavender-honey truffles.

"So," Aunt Nettie said casually, picking up a piping bag to help with the filling, "Saturday night, is it?"

"Don't start," I warned, though without much heat.

"I think it's wonderful," Bunny declared, carefully arranging dried lavender sprigs for decoration. "After everything that's happened, you deserve something sweet in your life that isn't chocolate."

"Though chocolate certainly doesn't hurt," Aunt Nettie added with a wink.

As we worked together in the sunlit kitchen, transforming simple ingredients into delicate confections, I felt a profound sense of rightness settle over me. The Easter mystery had been solved, justice had been served, and Sweetwater Springs was beginning the process of healing. And here, in the heart of Heavenly Confections, three women bound together by chocolate and survival were crafting something beautiful from the aftermath.

Like the perfect truffle—bitter chocolate transformed by careful hands into something exquisite—our ordeal had somehow yielded unexpected sweetness. New friendship with Bunny, who was blossoming beyond her clumsy beginnings into a truly gifted chocolatier. Renewed purpose for Aunt Nettie, whose fierce protection of our shop had reminded the town of her formidable spirit. And for me, a promising connection with James Morrison that might lead to something worth savoring slowly, appreciating each nuanced layer.

"You know," I said, piping a delicate swirl of white chocolate atop a finished truffle, "I think we should rename these 'New Beginnings' instead of just lavender-honey."

"Perfect," Aunt Nettie agreed. "And perhaps we should create a new signature collection. 'The Sleuthing Series'—chocolate mysteries waiting to be uncovered."

"As long as none of them are poisoned," Bunny added with a giggle.

"Absolutely not," I assured her with a laugh. "The only thing deadly about our chocolates from now on will be how impossible they are to resist."

As laughter filled the kitchen and morning sunlight streamed through the windows, I knew that whatever came next—for Sweetwater Springs, for Heavenly Confections, for all of us—would be faced together, with the same courage and determination that had carried us through the darkness of the past week.

The Chocolate Bunny Murders had tested us all, revealing strengths we hadn't known we possessed and connections we hadn't realized we needed. But like the finest chocolate, we had emerged from the heat transformed into something richer, more complex, and ultimately more satisfying than before.

I looked at the perfect rows of truffles before us—each one a small work of art, a testament to patience and skill and the magic that happens when simple ingredients come together in just the right way. Life, I reflected, wasn't so different. The bitter and the sweet, the smooth and the textured, all combining to create something worth savoring.

"To new beginnings," I said, raising a truffle in toast.

"To sweet justice," Aunt Nettie added with a twinkle in her eye.

"To Heavenly Confections," Bunny completed, "and all the chocolates yet to come."

As we clinked our truffles together in a most unconventional toast, I couldn't help but smile at the perfection of the moment. The Easter mystery was solved, but our story—like the finest handcrafted chocolate—was just beginning to reveal its most delicious possibilities.

THE END

Thank You to Readers

Dear Reader,

Thank you from the bottom of my heart for choosing "The Chocolate Bunny Murders" for your reading pleasure. I hope you enjoyed your visit to Sweetwater Springs and your time with Lee, Aunt Nettie, and Bunny as they solved their first mystery together.

Your support means the world to me. If you enjoyed their adventure, I would be incredibly grateful if you could take a moment to leave an honest review on Amazon. Your feedback not only helps other readers find my books but also provides invaluable insights that help me grow as a writer.

Whether you loved the story or found areas for improvement, I value your opinion. Every review, no matter how brief, makes a significant difference in an author's journey.

Thank you again for joining me in this sweet and mysterious adventure. I hope to welcome you back to Sweetwater Springs again soon!

With gratitude,

Holly Winters

Made in the USA
Columbia, SC
17 April 2025